Past

PRESENCE

Dorothy Topfer

Past Presence

First published in Australia by Dorothy Topfer 2021
www.dorothy.topfer.com

Copyright © Dorothy Topfer 2021
All Rights Reserved

 A catalogue record for this
book is available from the
National Library of Australia

ISBN: 978-0-6451559-0-7 (pbk)
ISBN: 978-0-6451559-1-4 (ebk)

Book cover photography by Sara Phemister © 2021

Typesetting and design by Publicious Book Publishing
Published in collaboration with Publicious Book Publishing
www.publicious.com.au

Dedicated to the Phemister family
whose magical home inspired this story.

Acknowledgements

Whenever I visited Sara, Al and their family, I would always say how their atmospheric home and its enchanted garden was the perfect setting for a story. So, with their kind permission, I sat down to write—and the story just flowed. I like to think it could have actually happened there—but who knows?

This story is entirely fictional and my own work, but I was honoured to be given some expert artistic advice from Freya Blackwood. Thank you, Freya. I love your illustrations and appreciate you sharing with me the mysteries of illustrating children's books. Any mistakes are my own.

I can't lay claim to the title. *Past Presence* is the result of inspired workshopping with my dear friend Annie Brent and my husband John.

Thank you also to my dear friends who are always encouraging me to keep writing – Karen, Alex and Lisa from our writers' group, Annie Robson and all the alumni from the Fiona McIntosh Masterclass, and of course Fiona McIntosh herself.

Thank you to everyone at Publicious Book Publishing Services, and to my editor Julie Guthrie at Say it Write, who polished this story to make it shine.

And finally, a warm and loving thank you to my family—especially my dear, and very patient, husband.

Prologue

One Hundred Years Ago (more or less)

The boy grunted from the effort of releasing the dead rabbit from the jaws of the rusty metal trap. Another one to add to the two rabbits already tied onto string around his waist. If he hurried back home, there might be enough time for his mother to cook the rabbits for tonight's meal.

The thought of a savoury meat stew made his stomach rumble in anticipation. He was forever hungry, and it wasn't because of growing pains—there just wasn't enough food to go around.

But there wasn't time to linger thinking about food. A quick glance around the clearing confirmed that it was getting late. The lengthening shadows and the golden glow of an imminent sunset made it clear that he had no time to spare. Securing the carcass to the string that encircled his waist, he set off down the worn path in the direction of home, whistling softly as he went.

It was the only home he had ever known. Not much to an outsider, but it was all he had. Bertie was small for his age—wiry and underfed. His large eyes, set in a bony face, peered out from under a straggle cut fringe. He was not terribly clean and was clad in little more than rags. His bare feet were tougher than the leather those fancy nobs wore on their feet when they came to town. He was small but tough. He had to be. In his ten years of life, he had already experienced more than most people many times his age.

Approaching the brick cottage by the riverside, he could already hear the quarrelsome sounds of his parents—his father's deep voice booming with accusation and threat. It was directed at his mother—as usual. His mother's tones were much softer, an attempt to deflect the rage. This was a futile activity, as Bertie knew only too well from past experiences.

Pa must have already been on the liquor Bertie thought. He paused, uncertain whether to proceed. His father, when enraged, was someone best avoided. But Bertie was the bearer of food. He glanced down at the rabbit carcasses hanging limp and bloody from his string belt. Surely this bounty of food would ease his way and ensure a welcome. Too late. His approach had been noticed by his younger siblings—two sisters and a brother—who were cowering on the front porch in a vain attempt to escape from the discord inside. With happy cries they came scampering towards Bertie, his youngest brother yelling out, 'Wait for me!' as he struggled to keep up.

His shout filled the momentary silence as those inside the cottage drew breath and noticed Bertie's arrival. The porch door squealed in protest as it was forced open, and Bertie's father appeared.

Face scowling, he did not observe his children with any affection. To him, they were a drain on his meagre finances and a distraction for his wife who, he believed, should be focused on attending to his needs. If he had his way, their children would have been drowned at birth like so many useless kittens.

'Where have you been you useless boy?' he roared at his approaching son.

Bertie untied the string belt and held up the three limp bodies for inspection. A sort of peace offering he hoped.

'Look Pa, three rabbits in the traps. Enough for a good meal for all of us. I'll just skin them and …'

Whack! The flat of an enormous hand hit Bertie on the side of his face, sending him sprawling into the dust. The rabbits, thrown in different directions from Bertie's fall, were gathered by the older of the two girls. Bertie, knowing what was coming, curled himself up into a ball, arms positioned protectively around his head.

The kicks that thumped into his body were accompanied by yells of abuse delivered in such a guttural tone it was difficult to make sense of them—if there was any sense to be had.

'No, No. Clive leave him. Leave him be for heaven's sake.' Bertie's mother rushed through the door heading towards her son.

Whack! Bertie's mother was hurled away, her body thudding into the thick timber post on the porch. Momentarily winded, she lay in a limp heap, gasping for breath with shuddering whimpers.

The kicking ceased. But that was only because a new method of attack had commenced. In one swift move, Bertie felt himself being dragged upright, two beefy hands grasping him by the shoulders, his father's face looming ominously close. The abuse continued—delivered in bespittled words overladen with the stink of alcohol. Bertie squirmed, but the grip tightened. Then, a sudden release as he was hurled away again.

Thud! Bertie hit the ground, his body landing at the foot of the stairs leading up to the porch. A dull crack—the sound of his head hitting the stone step—was the second last sound he heard. The last sound his mother's anguished screams as he took his final breath.

Chapter One

The person who rang no doubt meant well, but as their voice wittered on and on Deedee found it increasingly hard to pay attention. Her eyes were drawn to the scene outside her study window. The shards of light sparkling on the waves were urging her to end the call and join their revelry in the ocean. She turned her back and tried to focus on what was being said to her.

'Your aunt is incredibly lucky her turn was not any more serious and we got her into hospital as soon as we could. If she had spent the night outside on the porch steps, it could have been much worse. So fortunate the neighbour popped in and found her there.'

The caller—a doctor she thought—paused as if he expected her to agree. So as not to disappoint, Deedee allowed herself a small grunt to signify her accord.

The caller continued, 'We have run a number of tests. It would appear your aunt has had some sort of fainting episode, possibly heart related. But to be certain, she will need more tests and I would also recommend she consult a specialist. However, we are concerned about discharging her without some sort of care arrangement in place—at least for now—until we are all sure she can manage on her own. Your aunt is remarkably healthy for her age but given recent events, she has agreed with us that some extra help in the short term will be necessary.'

There was a pause as he drew a breath, as did Deedee. It was not hard to figure out what was about to be said.

'So, she has agreed that I ring you and see if it is possible for you to come down here and stay with her for a few weeks. If continuing care is needed, we can look at putting ongoing assistance in place or maybe even investigate whether there are any vacancies in our local aged care facility.'

Those last words did it. The decision was clear. Her aunt. Her independent, determined, and feisty aunt had no place living in an aged care facility. Not only would she go mad, but she would likely send all the other residents around the bend and make their lives a living hell. Deedee should know, she once lived with her.

Their relationship, in recent times, was civilised, almost affectionate. But the success of their relationship could well have been because they lived a safe distance apart—Deedee in the Northern Beaches, Sydney, and Great-Aunt Minnie in southern New South Wales. It was close enough to permit weekend visits, but far enough to ensure they each had their own space and were free to live individual lives that were only loosely connected. For years now that arrangement had worked for them both. But now, it could all be under threat. Still, she reassured herself. The doctor had made it clear that what was planned was only intended to be a short-term arrangement and for that reason, Deedee hoped it would be manageable for both of them.

A quick mental review of her immediate commitments made her realise there was nothing that could not be managed long distance. Her housemate would keep the garden watered and would most likely welcome having the house to himself. Her work—well, she could do that anywhere. As an illustrator of children's books, all she needed was the paper, pencils, ink, and paints she used to produce her work. She could be anywhere in the world and still be productive, so long as she had Internet access. Her current commitment—illustrating for a book entitled, *Wanderings with Wendy, the not so Wicked Witch* was almost complete—only a few more *W's* to grapple with. There was also no longer any partner from whom she had to drag herself away, and for once her unattached status appeared to be an advantage.

'Of course. I can arrange to stay with my aunt. How soon do you need me?'

'As soon as possible—in the next day or so would be great. We'll keep her here until you arrive, and we'll maybe do a few more tests and organise some physio. How about the day after tomorrow? Can you do that?'

'I'll try. I'll see what I can sort out and get back to you to confirm.'

The call ended and Deedee once again turned towards the window and contemplated the beach scene on display. People, happy in their own activities and life, paraded before her—couples, families, some with various types of dogs—large and small. All were busy—running, swimming, cycling, or just simply lying at ease on a towel on the sand—all seemingly content with their lot. Meanwhile, Deedee was set apart, cocooned in her own little world, separated by this pane of glass. Until she had received that phone call, this self-contained little world had been enough. Her skill with illustrations was both recognised and highly praised, and she had sufficient work lined up into the foreseeable future to ensure a regular income. But if she was to be completely honest with herself, it was maybe no longer giving her the challenging artistic satisfaction that she craved.

The rest of the afternoon was taken up making arrangements to leave. It wasn't until late afternoon that she found time for one last swim, followed by a solitary walk along the beach. As she meandered along the shoreline, Deedee found herself wondering what had really happened to her aunt. The doctor had only given her the bare details, yet one comment resonated with her—that her aunt had been found by the front steps of the porch. Could she have tripped and fallen? After all, the cottage was incredibly old and rather dilapidated, and accidents could happen at any time. Perhaps it was carelessness rather than some underlying health condition that caused the accident. In a way that very thought gave her some comfort. It might mean her stay would be so much shorter.

The next day, with her little car crammed full of clothes,

paints, and every gourmet food product she thought could possibly come in useful, she was going to the country after all. Deedee left the Northern Beaches and joined the stream of traffic heading out of Sydney. Once she reached the Hume Highway, the traffic cleared, and she drove south.

Chapter Two

Every kilometre of the road was known to her. After all, this was a journey she had made countless times. Deedee turned up the music and slipped into a state of being where all she thought about was the demands of driving safely, and the pleasure of singing along to her favourite songs.

To keep with family tradition, she made a quick stop at Berrima. This allowed enough time for a toilet break, and coffee and cake at her favourite café. Then she was back on the road. If all went well and barring any unforeseen mishaps, she would be there in just two more hours of tedious freeway driving. Her own music had now been abandoned for the dubious pleasures of the local radio station. Deedee listened vaguely in a forlorn attempt to catch up on what was the latest gossip in her old hometown. Dominating the airwaves, reports covered the impact of the drought, record prices at a recent sheep sale, and some development controversy. A discussion about a proposed residential redevelopment to be constructed along the river in her childhood town caught her attention. Could this be somewhere near her aunt's home? The report finished with Deedee none the wiser as to its whereabouts, but she made a mental note to find out more.

The afternoon shadows were lengthening by the time she approached her aunt's hometown. Turning off the freeway, Deedee drove slowly through the outskirts trying to focus on the road. But she found herself distracted by the new semirural developments that she passed. Each time she visited, and it wasn't too often these days, she found it disconcerting that the country town she remembered from her childhood was disappearing, rapidly becoming subsumed by new subdivisions and modern housing. Yet, in the old part, the wide streets that had been laid down by the early settlers to accommodate the wagons and drays, remained. The streetscape was a mix of old two storey buildings with wide verandahs—a relic from another century—now interspersed with large modern structures housing mega grocery stores. A convenience she was sure, but did they have to be so ugly?

Her aunt's home was located not far off the main street but was still very close to the centre of town. Turning left before she reached the river, Deedee drove a short way and turned right. This road was much narrower and only lasted a few hundred metres before it petered off into little more than a track, and then nothing—any further progress blocked by choking undergrowth. There wasn't much down here—her aunt's cottage and two other neighbours. In many ways, this part of the town had been overlooked by progress, hence the dirt track and lack of kerbside gutters. Deedee suspected that somehow this was exactly how these residents liked it to be.

She stopped her car at the end of the road, got out, stretched, and glanced around. Everything looked much the same as it did when she last visited earlier this year, some nine months ago. It was the same except for maybe being slightly more overgrown. The hedge that lined the road, screening out all else, was even higher and stragglier than when she was last here. The white picket gate that was the only entry to the yard from the street, appeared as though it was in urgent need of repair, hanging crookedly off its hinges. Taking a deep breath, Deedee manoeuvred the gate and made her way into the garden.

The garden was as it had always been—a welcoming oasis removed from reality. Birds sang and small animals made their presence known with their furtive rustling in the undergrowth. Noise from nearby traffic and other people fell away, blocked by the dense vegetation. Just like when she was a little girl, Deedee felt as if she had stepped back in time and had entered some magical kingdom where she would be kept safe and nurtured.

A path made of randomly placed stone with red brick edging curved around the garden beds that were in early spring display. Daffodils, bluebells, and blue and yellow violas clustered and competed for space in a garden that was crammed with other plants, many of which were unknown to Deedee. The overall impression however, was of colour and vigour as all the plants celebrated the arrival of sunshine and spring warmth. Scattered plantings of tall trees could be seen, presumably intended to provide shelter for the garden from inclement winds. Towards the southern boundary, was a row of pine trees of venerable age. Through the plantings Deedee could see the tin roof of her aunt's cottage, hidden from view even from inside the yard, only revealing itself bit by bit with each step she took. Closer to the house, and on the town side of the land, there was a massed planting of elms which, judging from their enormous girth, were much older than Deedee.

As she brushed her way along the path, Deedee muttered to herself about the urgent need to cut back the undergrowth. She found the current appearance of the garden unexpected. Her aunt had certainly always encouraged vigorous growth in her garden—her pride and joy—but never to this extent. All through her childhood, Deedee's aunt had delighted in pottering around in her garden each day doing a bit of this and a bit of that. But she would never have permitted things to deteriorate to such an extent. With growing unease, Deedee wondered what had been happening to result in such neglect, and why her aunt had failed to divulge these changes during their weekly telephone conversations.

Reaching the end of the path, she paused to consider the cottage. Now fully revealed, it sprawled across the land like an organic being—something that had grown and expanded over time to accommodate the demands of generations of families. The original four room cottage that had housed its early inhabitants, was clearly visible from the front of the house that faced the river. Behind that structure, a rambling extension had been built some hundred years ago, to which a two-storey annexe had been added by subsequent owners. All in all, the house had the appearance of a cobbled together letter 'U'. Built from random weatherboard, red brick and stone, it was haphazard in its charm. An upstairs area that overlay both the extension and annexe, accommodated the bedrooms—each with a dormer window, like so many eyebrows. It resembled a house that was straight out of one of the many fairytales Deedee had loved as a child. No wonder she had fallen in love with this cottage the first time she saw it when she was a little over nine years old. As she stood there drinking in the charm of her favourite cottage, the one so often replicated in her illustrations, Deedee wondered why she had ever thought it was a good idea to leave.

Pausing underneath the overhanging eave by the door, she felt around for the door key which, as usual, was hanging on a hook by the hat rack. It wasn't really the official front door. That was the battered door on the porch, facing the river. The real front door was only ever used in summer as a means to access the porch where Deedee and her aunt would often sit at leisure, enjoying a gin and tonic in the cool of the evening. Or where they would greet those visitors who might have entered the garden from the pathway that ran alongside the river.

It may not have been the official front door, but this side door was the door that was used every day. The boots flanked each side, the hats and coats that hung from the nearby hooks all testament to this door being the preferred point of entry.

Deedee unlocked the door and pushed hard on it. With a scraping sound, the door grudgingly permitted access. Deedee made yet another mental note—the door also needed fixing. There was clearly something going on with those hinges.

Propping the door open, Deedee moved inside. With her aunt still in hospital she thought it would be worthwhile getting the home warm and comfortable before she brought her home. And maybe stocking up with some food too. She knew how rarely her aunt bothered with things such as food and expected there would be little to eat in the house.

A miaow alerted her to the presence of another. In a patch of late afternoon sunshine, sat a black cat watching her with wary golden eyes. It made hopeful noises in anticipation of some food.

'Hello Merlin. You poor thing. All alone here? I bet you are wondering where your mistress is. I hope someone has been keeping an eye on you. Let's see if there is any food for you and then I'll light the fire. You'd like that, wouldn't you?'.

Deedee interpreted the rumbling purr in response as consent to her proposal. With his black tail held high, gently wafting to and fro, Merlin led the way down the corridor through a dining/sitting area and into a galley kitchen that looked out onto the garden. There was no need to try and locate the cat food because Merlin, by sitting in front of one of the cupboards, made it clear where his food was stored.

With food spooned out onto a saucer for an appreciative cat, Deedee then turned her attention to the heating. The chill seeping out of the walls and up through the floorboards made it obvious that the house had not been heated for some time. In Deedee's experience, the slow combustion heater in the chimney space of the dining/sitting area was usually on slow burn, which ensured an ambient warmth pervaded downstairs. Other forms of heating were of course scattered throughout the house. This was an old house after all and like everything else, improvements in heating had happened incrementally in accordance with the needs of subsequent generations of occupants. Each improvement added to the existing arrangements, none of which were ever removed. Deedee knew she would find electric heaters in each bedroom and in the bathroom, which were good for short-term relief. In the main sitting room, a rather grand stone fireplace remained from days long past but was only used on special occasions when the house was full of visitors and good cheer. But today the slow combustion heater would suffice. Of course, the repurposed copper next to the heater was empty of firewood. With a sigh she turned towards the door and headed outside to the wood heap located behind the house. Several trips later, Deedee had amassed sufficient wood to fuel the fire. All that remained was to locate some kindling. With so many trees in the garden, finding some dead twigs proved to be easy—the old trees near the side gate provided sufficient goods for her needs. Deedee was so focused on the task at hand, she failed to notice the scraping noise of the gate as someone entered the yard. A cough and a voice saying, 'Here. Let me help,' was the first she knew that someone else was nearby. She turned with a start and promptly whacked her head on an overhanging branch.

'Ouch,' she said dropping the kindling she had been holding and with both hands, she grabbed the side of her head.

'Ouch,' she said again. 'That hurt. Do you mind? You gave me a fright.' She glared at the stranger.

He smiled back at her, almost as if he knew her. Did she know him? Nope.

'Sorry about that. I didn't realise you were right behind the gate. I was driving past and saw a car I didn't recognise and thought I should check in on the house. What with Minnie still being in hospital and all I just thought I should make sure everything is okay. Oh, and give Merlin a bit of a snack. He's such a pig, but you probably already know that! Here let me get that,' he said as Deedee bent to retrieve the sticks of wood.

'Here for long?' he asked as they both continued to gather the kindling head-to-head.

It was obvious that he knew her. Looking closely at his face next to hers, Deedee was puzzled as to who he might be. Obviously a local. About her age. He was dressed in the sort of attire a person would wear if they were focused entirely on outdoor manual labour—worn, dirty, stained jeans; steel-capped, lace-up boots, and a khaki shirt displaying some sort of logo. If she peered closely, she could make out an embroidered circle with a stylised green leaf inside it, above which were the embroidered words, *Frost Landscaping*. Well, that didn't clarify things at all. She still didn't know who he was. Deedee looked up at a face laughing down at her. He knew exactly what was going on. The wretch and how embarrassing! A wave of heat rushed over her face as Deedee struggled with her emotions—

embarrassment coupled with anger that her solitude had been disturbed by this stranger who was not only crouched way too close to her but was now laughing at her with eyes as bright green in colour as the spring growth that surrounded them.

'It's okay if you don't remember me Deedee. After all, it's been years since we last spoke. Come on, let's get this kindling inside and get the fire going. I suppose that's what you had in mind.'

With a calloused and grimy hand, he helped her upright and followed her along the path, chatting about this and that as they went. He clearly expected no response as he spoke without a break.

'Minnie will be pleased to see you. She's had a bit of a rough time since Alice died earlier this year. I suppose she doesn't want you to worry, but we've all been a bit concerned about her wellbeing—not just her physical state but ... she also just doesn't seem to be herself. I guess that could be grief and all. I have been trying to pop in regularly for a chat on my way home and of course I keep trying to encourage her to cut this jungle back a bit, but she won't hear of it! Still, I keep trying. Here let me ...' he said as he held the screen door open for Deedee.

As Deedee busied herself with lighting the fire, the stranger crouched and engaged with Merlin who expressed his appreciation by gently purring and ingratiating himself around the stranger's legs.

'Merlin, you old rogue you. I can tell you have already been fed by your lack of complaint.'

He looked up with a humorous gleam in his eyes. 'Remember me yet? I probably looked a bit different in our old school days. More hair.' And with that he dislodged his baseball cap which, although somewhat obscured by sweat and stains, displayed the same logo as the one on his shirt. The hat, now removed, revealed a closely cropped head.

Deedee stared at him intently. There was something familiar about him. Perhaps if she could picture this man a bit younger with longer hair, it might help. Yes! It definitely did help. An image of a young boy with a thatch of wild, straw-coloured hair, grinning back at her with the same smile, sprung into her mind.

11

'Harry, is that you? Harry Frost?' He nodded and she continued, 'No way! It's been ages since I saw you last. And you expect me to remember you?'

'Well, I managed not to forget.'

'But you've changed so much. Taller and ...' She struggled to put into words her initial impression of calmness and maturity—not characteristics she remembered from the Harry of her childhood.

'So grown up ...' she concluded rather lamely.

'Yeah, I know.' His sigh was softened with a smile and a twinkle from his beautiful eyes. 'It happens to us all—the need to be responsible and earn a living.' He gestured at the logo on his shirt.

'You never moved on? Left town?'

'Only for long enough to study horticulture, but then I came straight back. There seemed no reason to be anywhere else. Mind you, on a good day I'm in the car and heading straight to the coast and the surf. Luckily, it's not too far away. But Mum and Dad are here, and them and my brother need a hand with the farm from time to time. Although that wasn't the reason I returned. It's just there was no real reason to stay away. I like it here and it suits me. There's heaps of work for me. And you? Will you be here for a while?'

Deedee shrugged.

'I have no idea. So much depends on Minnie and what she needs.'

'Good luck with that! She's a stubborn old thing. Chances are she'll tell you she needs nothing!'

Chapter Three

'I can manage perfectly well on my own.'

The delivery of those words might have been with a querulous tone of voice, but there was no mistaking the determination in the elderly woman's voice or in her steely gaze as she glared at her visitor.

'There really was no need for that meddlesome doctor to call you,' Minnie continued. Her gaze softened as she considered the young woman standing apprehensively before her.

'But then again, it is a treat to see you, so I suppose a short visit is a good idea. Until I am up and about—a day or two at that—and by then you'll have had enough of your old aunt I suppose. Come here, give me a kiss and help me up so we can get out of this place before they change their minds and keep me in any longer.'

As Deedee embraced her aunt and helped her to her feet, she became aware of her fragility. It had been some time since she had paid close attention to Minnie. Her rushed visit at Christmas had been a chaotic few days, crammed full of frivolity and celebration. The return trip only a few weeks afterwards had been too full of sorrow for her to expect her aunt to be other than frail. But now, fussing over Minnie, taking her arm and helping her walk out of the hospital and into the car, Deedee realised there was much less of her aunt than there used to be. The navy drill trousers draped over her twig-like legs and she noticed that the fine woollen jumper she wore bagged over her aunt's skinny frame. Deedee frowned. Had her aunt been like this last time she saw her at Alice's funeral? She cast her mind back and recalled a much more robust aunt those few short months ago. Was this changed appearance the direct result of grief or was there something else going on?

But there was no mistaking the energy in her aunt's voice as she supervised Deedee's driving.

'Not too fast now. Turn right here at the roundabout. Careful. Mind those potholes and watch out for old Mrs Bromfield.'

Deedee slowed her car to permit Mrs Bromfield to complete her crossing, moving at a stately pace, preceded by her geriatric poodle. She tried not to let her frustration show, yet somehow her aunt must have sensed the tension in the air.

'I suppose that will be me in the future. No smelly old dog though, but probably reliant on a Zimmer frame. I wonder if anyone will be kind enough to stop for me like you have just done or if the young ones will keep on going and mow me down. Now there's a thought. Going out in a blaze of glory squished by the younger generation. I'd certainly make headlines then.'

Despite herself Deedee found herself snorting with laughter. Trust her aunt to turn the situation around.

'I doubt it Minnie. More likely you'll have one of those hot little motorised scooters—bright red with fluttering flags, and you'll be the one running down those people that don't get out of *your* way!'

'Not a bad suggestion at all Deedee dear.' Minnie leaned back into the car seat, arthritic hands clasped in her lap, and glanced dreamily out of the window.

'Perhaps I need to go scooter shopping while you are here.'

It was soon very clear that the brief burst of energy that had engulfed Minnie was only sufficient to get her from hospital to home. It was obvious Minnie was exhausted by the way she leaned on her niece as they slowly walked down the garden path. Once inside, Deedee settled her aunt in the shabby armchair that flanked the heater. Clearly a popular place to rest, and not a seat Merlin was keen to vacate—even for his beloved mistress. As Deedee shooed Merlin away, his glare needed no translation. His message was communicated clearly—*I was here first.*

'Never mind Merlin,' said Deedee, taking pity on him. 'You have your mistress home. The fire is lit and how about I give you some more food?'

Food works every time, she thought, *whether for humans or animals*. With that in mind she turned to her aunt.

'Tea or coffee?' she asked.

'Or something stronger? Now you mention it, most definitely something stronger Deedee dear. In the freezer you'll find some gin and with a bit of luck there might still be some tonic in the fridge.'

'And not much else Aunt,' said Deedee, fossicking in the freezer. She located a half full bottle of gin and triumphantly waved it in the air. 'Speaking of the fridge, I have already done some shopping as all you seem to have in this house is cat food and tonic—and of course, this gin. What have you been eating?'

'Not much.' Minnie's voice deepened and her emotion was clear. 'I really haven't been hungry. Since Alice died there hasn't seemed to be much point. Nothing worse than eating alone. Sorry Merlin. In this context you don't count. And I just can't seem to get the hang of cooking for one. The neighbours have been wonderful, bringing me casseroles and the like, and that young Harry, he often pops by with a little something for me—you know, a cake or some bread rolls or some fancy deli treats. But ...' Her voice slowed. 'It just doesn't seem worth the fuss and bother anymore.'

'Never mind that,' Deedee said briskly. 'I'm here now. Let me fuss over you. It'll be fun to have someone to practise my cooking on. But be warned, there's no guarantee that what I create will be edible. How about we start with something simple tonight? Scrambled eggs and bacon suit you?'

'Simple is good and that sounds wonderful Deedee dear.'

Minnie took several appreciative sips of her drink and relaxed back into the joy of being at home. As she did so she listened to the tinny sounds of pots and pans being thudded onto the stove. Deedee always was a bit full on her aunt recalled. Occasional out-of-tune singing emanated from the kitchen, singing clearly not her strong point. Minnie took another sip of her drink—a strong gin and tonic, just the way she liked it—and she smiled. Perhaps things weren't so bad after all now that she had company—live company that is. The other residents in this house just got on her nerves and she wished they would go away. Minnie glanced down at Merlin who, in prime position in front of the fire, was focused on his grooming.

'Fat lot of good you are Merlin. You call yourself a witch's cat.'

His grooming paused as he looked up and contemplated his mistress with eyes glowing golden citrine. Sometimes Minnie was convinced that Merlin understood every word she said, and this appeared to be one such occasion.

'Yes, you. I expect you to take care of our girl and make sure no harm comes to her. I'm not convinced this is a good idea for Deedee to be living back here, although her company is most welcome. But things have changed. Something is in the air and we no longer have Alice for protection. It's up to you and me, Merlin my friend,' she concluded as she took another sip.

Merlin contemplated Minnie for a second more, then resumed his grooming as if he failed to see what all the fuss was about. And it was possible he was correct Minnie thought. Maybe animals' instincts are much more reliable than those of fallible humans.

They decided that dinner would be so much more delicious if it was eaten on their knees in front of the fire—and it was. In companionable silence they both concentrated on their meal, agreeing afterwards that they hadn't realised how hungry they were. A quick flick through the TV channels confirmed there was nothing worth watching and they each relaxed into their evening activities— Minnie untangling a knitting project that appeared to have been appropriated by Merlin while she had been in hospital, and Deedee opening a sketch book preparatory to start a drawing. At her aunt's raised eyebrow, Deedee explained.

'It's for the commission I'm working on. Illustrations for this children's book. It's called something like *Wanderings with Wendy the not so Wicked Witch*. I'm almost done and to be honest I am a bit over Wendy. Witch or not she is a bit goody two shoes. And for some reason the author is very keen on Wendy interacting with anything beginning with a W. Illustrations involve wombats, wolves, warthogs to name a few, but they are not my speciality. I'm much better with pretty stuff so I have snuck in a few rainbows and even a unicorn. But I suspect the editor will insist I remove those. At least young Wendy has a dog. It was going to be a West Highland Terrier. Yep, a 'W' word. But now they are a bit too worried that it is a bit too *Wizard of Oz*. So, I've convinced them to let me try and draw a dog that isn't too similar for this illustration, and I need to do a few rough sketches. So, I might as well start now,' she concluded, waving a pencil in the air.

'Welsh corgis could be an option, starting with a 'W' and all that.' suggested her aunt.

'Maybe. But that could be risky. The monarchists might decide we are implying the Queen is a witch!'

'A good witch mind you.'

With a laugh, Deedee settled into her drawing. The only sounds were the scratch of a pencil, the muttered curses as Minnie struggled to untangle yet another knot, and the purr of a contented cat. From time to time there was a crackle and thud from the fire as the wood settled into place. Outside night-time had fallen. The garden was bathed in the translucent glow of a full moon, and it was cold as would be expected for this time of year. The air was still, and a frost had started to settle, coating the trees in a shimmer of white icy crystals. The two women and one cat were at ease inside in the warmth, unaware of the figure peering furtively in through the window. Only the cat noticed. His purring stopped as he looked up alertly at the intruder.

'What's up Merlin?' Minnie noticed almost straight away. 'Do you need to go outside?'

With a shake, the black cat dismissed the suggestion. Didn't the mistress know how cold it was outside? Whoever or whatever was out there would just have to manage on their own. They were safe and warm in here. Even a cat knows when not to mess with trouble, and he was certain that whatever was out there meant them no good.

Minnie yawned and started to put away her knitting.

'Well, that's me done for the night. I think I will head off to bed. No Deedee, don't get up. If I take it slowly, I can manage. I'll sleep downstairs in the spare room until I feel up to tackling the stairs. There's a heater in there and I'll be fine. Your old room is made up and you won't be disturbed by me up there, although I give you no promises about this pesky cat. He does tend to patrol during the night. A bit like a night watchman. Nonetheless, please make sure the back door is locked before you go to bed. Just a precaution as I'm sure most people don't even know we exist behind that hedge. But you never can be too sure. Goodnight Deedee dear. Don't get up, and make sure you sleep in as I certainly intend to!'

Slowly, Minnie eased herself out of the armchair, then with tentative steps she headed in the direction of the bedroom located down the hall adjacent the bathroom.

Merlin and Deedee contemplated her slow progress. Then, as if satisfied that Minnie would successfully make it to the bedroom under her own steam, they both resumed their own tasks: Deedee working on yet another drawing, the previous one having been rejected, and the black cat repositioning himself, belly facing the fire to absorb maximum warmth.

Sometime later, with fingers cramping, Deedee paused and considered what she had done. Not a bad image of Wendy—a side view of her leaning over to rescue the dog from some sort of cage. Deedee supposed it was something a not-so-wicked witch would do. Behind the image of Wendy, was a cottage shaded by overhanging trees—a cottage Deedee now realised closely resembled the one in which she was residing that night. Peeking out from behind the trees was an array of fairy forest folk. Not quite in accordance with what she had been instructed to draw, but it was still rather satisfying for the artist. With her head to one side, Deedee contemplated her creation and was rather pleased with her effort.

'Not too bad. Maybe tomorrow I'll paint this up and see how it looks. Who knows, maybe they'll approve. I mean she is a witch after all, so surely we can surround her with a few other magical creatures.'

With a yawn and a stretch, Deedee stood up. Mindful of her

aunt's instructions, she locked the side door, wandered down the corridor to the front door and checked that it was also locked. It was. No surprise there as that door was very rarely used. A quick glance into the old sitting room to confirm all was still as it was last time she was there. She paused. Was that a shadow moving across the wooden floor—a shadow that appeared to be created by something blocking the moonlight flooding in through the window? As Deedee moved into the room, the shadow also moved, leaving the room bathed in the light of the full moon again.

Deedee shook her head. Did she just imagine that? After all she was tired, and it had been a long day. This house had always been a bit strange. Maybe it was only the light playing tricks on her. Gently closing the sitting room door, she turned to head for her bedroom. As she turned out the corridor light, she glanced behind her, remembering the first time she saw that sitting room. She couldn't recall much detail, as it was over twenty years ago, but she could still recall the strange feeling and the sensation that she was not alone. A bit like now ...

Chapter Four

Twenty Years Ago

It had been a long day but at last, they were almost there—back at Minnie's home that is. The place that was once a loving home for the little girl dozing in the back seat was no longer—now a charred and smouldering wreck soon to be razed to the ground. There was no hope for the two inhabitants on that unfortunate and fateful night.

The drive back from Sydney had been interminable and silent. The child did not speak—she had barely spoken since that terrible night when all that was familiar and loving to her, was consigned to flames. Her parents and her pets consumed by a voracious fire.

A quirk of fate had saved her. That night her best friend at the time was having a birthday sleepover. 'Sleepover' wasn't really an accurate description of the event as it was not until past midnight when the anxious parents could settle the overexcited children enough for them to sleep. The girl was still asleep at 9:00 am when the police knocked on the door to deliver the news of the grim discovery. Finding her had been a challenge for the local constabulary. They were initially convinced that everyone had perished in the flames. It wasn't until a vigilant neighbour, having spotted her leaving in her party clothes, suggested that the child might have gone elsewhere. It was only then that hopes were raised that she might have survived.

What following was horrifying—the shock, the grief, the frantic search for any relatives who could lay claim to this child. This all played out in the media—the press, TV and radio. A great-aunt was finally located, and she dashed to Sydney to assume responsibility for this forlorn and forsaken little waif.

As the outskirts of the dusty township came into view, the child stirred. She stretched with both arms aloft before placing her thumb firmly in her mouth and gazing around. The street was straight and wide, the houses uniform in their timber and brick construction, steep pitched roofs and front porches rising from the straight concrete paths by way of identical twin steps. Further along they traversed the shopping strip—wide verandahed, double-fronted shops, separated by the two-storey facades of the more affluent retailers—the butcher, the chemist, the newsagent, the haberdashery, and of course, the pub.

'Almost there,' her newly discovered relative said in a voice a little too bright, while looking up into the rear-view mirror to see if there was any reaction from the silent being in the back seat.

No reaction.

'Just around this corner and down the lane.'

Still no response.

They turned left and followed another wide street—tree lined and shady—before turning right into what at first seemed to be another driveway as it was narrow and overgrown. A dusty and rutted lane, it led past several cottages and then terminated— or maybe it was terminated by an overgrowth of trees, bushes, and the odd blackberry bush.

'Here we are. Home at last,' the woman said, sighing with relief as she reached to unbuckle her seatbelt.

'Come on then. Let's get you out of the car and inside.'

The child finally reacted. Get out? To where and inside what? She could see nothing. Where was the house? Could it be a tree house? For trees was all she could see before her. With her seatbelt undone, she clambered out of the car and gazed around searching for the 'home' that awaited her.

'This way Deedee dear.'

Her great-aunt led the way. She headed directly for the wall of shrubbery, pushing a tendril of a leafy climbing plant out of her way as she progressed along a path of randomly placed stones, edged with crumbling bricks. With a push and a shove of the greenery, a gate was revealed and opened. The child followed, stepping warily into the green lit space.

The path continued, curving past raised garden beds of flourishing plants. The child, barely nine years old, had no knowledge of the botanical names of the plants. But she could appreciate the colour and fragrance of the bounty of massed blooms that crowded around her. She could hear the birds' songs that celebrated life in this garden, and she could see butterflies flitting away, disturbed by her arrival. The darkness that had enveloped her in recent days, lightened. After all, this was once her mother's home—when she was a young woman, she lived here for a while with her aunt, only leaving to marry the child's father. Maybe in some very tenuous way, this also connected her to this place. A new home. The home she had left behind was now a pile of blackened timber. All she wanted to do at this moment was block out all recollection.

Another woman stood in the house. She held the screen door open and observed their arrival with a fixed and anxious gaze. Deedee watched her aunt greet this other woman with a hug, a kiss, and a whispered confidence. They both looked towards the child and, with fixed smiles meant to be reassuring, they gently beckoned her forwards. The child tightened her grip on her only remaining toy—a battered teddy bear that was a gift to her at birth—now moving forward into this new life with her.

Over a dinner of what these two women considered child-friendly food—rissoles, mashed potato and gravy—Deedee solemnly considered the two adults who would now be responsible for her care. She had already inspected her new home and while finding the haphazard arrangement of rooms, wonky doors, and creaky floors puzzling, it somehow also felt like a home she could come to like. Especially that cat—a black cat called Merlin who had been shadowing her every move. But when it came to these two adults, she was not so sure. The one called Alice was all colour and movement—her attire a random assortment of items, in rainbow colours, that fluttered with her every move. Her long hair was plaited into a coronet on her head and was secured with a mountain of bobby pins. Yet even so, the hair seemed determined to slip free and escape. Her every move incorporated a need to secure the rebel hair by removing and reattaching one or several bobby pins, talking as she did so, sometimes incomprehensibly as her words were obscured by her teeth gripping the bobby pins. But she seemed friendly and interested in Deedee and her wellbeing. She said she was an artist and invited Deedee to inspect her latest work and maybe try her own hand at painting. Maybe …

Her great-aunt—call me 'Minnie' but real name 'Minerva'. To Deedee that name sounded like the name of a posh serving dish. And posh she was. With a cut-glass accent so different to that of Deedee's dad, and with such close attention to Deedee's table etiquette, she wasn't sure how she would be able to satisfy her high standards. Her little hands clutched the knife and fork. This was all so strange. Once, in that other life that was no longer, she would have been sitting at a tiny table in the kitchen with her mother and father, laughing, eating whatever was put in front of her, and basking in the adoring regard of both her parents. No one watching *how* she ate or *what* she ate. No one caring if she stayed at the table or not. And no such thing as a serviette. She looked down at the starched cloth lying across her lap like some sort of shroud and shuddered. The cat rubbed against her chair, looking up at her as if to reassure and encourage Deedee to persevere and take another mouthful of dinner. It was not the pasta she was used to, and it contained more meat than she had ever encountered, but the potato with the gravy, she thought she might just be able to swallow.

After dinner she was instructed to sit in the front room in front of the fire and read a picture book while Minnie and Alice washed up.

'No need to help us tonight,' they both assured her. 'You must be tired. Just rest now. Merlin will keep you company. We'll be with you very soon with a mug of hot chocolate. You'll like that, won't you?'

Maybe. She was not so sure. Like an automaton, she followed

Minnie into the sitting room, perched herself on the brown velvet lounge, and permitted her aunt to drape her in some fusty handknitted rug of violent multi-coloured hues. A book was then placed in her hands.

'There child. This was a book your mother used to love. Have a look at it and we will both be back with you shortly. You should be warm enough with the fire and the lap rug.'

The open fire snapped and crackled, flames flaring and falling. Every now and then a gust of smoke would waft into the room—indicating that the direction of the wind was less than ideal—filling the room with the fragrance of eucalyptus. The child pulled the blanket closer and stared deeply into the flickering flames. Her eyelids fluttered. Surrendering to her weariness, she lay back and snuggled into the comfort of the pillowy lounge. The black cat jumped up and nestled into the space made by the angle of her bent knees. All too soon she was asleep. Not fully asleep, but in a sort of doze where resting was possible while the subconscious remained on the lookout for unexpected danger.

A whispering, a consultation between two people, interrupted her rest. As the whispering grew in intensity and volume, it permeated her consciousness. Had Alice and Minnie returned to the room, washing up chores completed? No, the voices were not full of energy like theirs. These were more like the sound of rustling leaves. They were initially incomprehensible, but the more she listened the easier it was to decipher the subject matter under discussion. They were talking about her—Deedee—but they didn't know her name.

With eyes scrunched tightly closed, she listened intently.

'But who is she?' said one in a trembling tone.

'I don't care who she is. She could be the Queen of England for all I care. She is in our room and without our permission,' said another in a complaining voice.

'Not only that. But look at her face. She is filthy. Must be a street urchin the cat dragged in. I blame the cat.'

Through barely opened eyes, obscured to some extent by her thick black eyelashes, Deedee tried to identify the source of the conversation. There was no one else in the room. Just her and a happily purring cat. No, wait a minute. What was that fuzziness by the fire? Her eyes opened a fraction more and she stared intently at the wall beside the fireplace. Like the other walls in the sitting room, it was a delight. It was covered in a wallpaper that must have been in vogue many years ago—a cornucopia of flowers, ivy and berries—fussy and overdone in both style and in colour. Yet, as Deedee peered at this wall, she could see the pattern wavering, lines blurring as the pattern faded. From the wallpaper emerged the heads and shoulders of two women from times gone by, hair piled up on their heads, and shawls wrapped tightly around their bony shoulders. Peering intently at her, they continued their conversation.

'It must be the fault of that Minerva woman and her cat. Always bringing waifs and strays into the house. Well, I won't stand for it,' declaimed the taller one—the one with the stronger, crosser voice.

'Don't be too rash sister dear,' the one with the wavering voice responded. 'She looks to be only young and maybe she needs a place of refuge, like we all did once. Let's not scare her off yet.'

'That's quite enough you two,' said Aunt Minnie, suddenly appearing in the doorway wiping her hands dry with a tea towel.

'Don't even think of trying your antics on with this child or you will have me to answer to.'

'Ah Minerva,' said the grim-faced one. 'Cicely and I were just concerned that our special room was at risk of being overrun by riff raff. No doubt you will be removing your latest stray before she stains the furniture with her filth.'

'As I said, that's quite enough. Where is your compassion? This so called 'stray' is one of ours. Her mother was my niece and young Deedee here needs our care.'

'Was?' asked the one with the softer voice.

'Yes. Was,' her aunt responded. 'Both she and her husband died in a house fire. Deedee has no one else to care for her. We, and that includes you two, are all the family she has now.'

'Burned. Like a witch?'

'Yes. Just so,' replied her aunt grimly. 'But that's enough of that now. Let's leave that discussion for another day.'

Minnie turned and contemplated her great niece lying tense and still on the lounge. She smiled.

'Deedee, I know you are awake and listening. Don't pretend. You can't fool me. Please let me introduce you to Eloise and Cicely who, by my calculations, lived in this house a long time ago and for some reason still like to linger. Strictly speaking, they may not be our relatives, but because they seem to want to share the house with us, I like to think of them as being part of our family. Really though, if they are to be included in our family, they should be much more polite than they have been just now. Age is no excuse. Nor is being dead for that matter. Please say hello to them and maybe, just maybe, they might find it in themselves to be civil.'

Deedee, sitting upright, dislodged the cat who made his displeasure known by giving a yowl and stalking away over to the fire, where he proceeded to groom all the while regarding the entertainment with his golden eyes.

'Hello,' said Deedee in a hesitant voice. After all, she had never been introduced to dead people before so she was unsure as to what the proper etiquette should be.

'Pleased to meet you. I'm sorry if I disturbed you. I'll try to be quieter in future … and cleaner,' she added, conscious of the remains of dinner still smeared on her face.

A grunt was the only acknowledgement Deedee received.

'Ladies,' Aunt Minnie warned in an ominous tone.

'Oh, very well then,' said the cranky one, who Deedee now understood was the one known as Eloise.

'Welcome to our home child. Please remember, we are incredibly old and don't like to be disturbed. You may enter our sitting room, but only with permission. You see, we are rather busy.'

'So much to do,' the one known as Cicely added. 'Our painting keeps us busy. See, there is some of our work on the walls over there. Papa enjoys them so.'

Deedee looked around and observed a collection of framed

watercolours hanging at random on the busy wallpaper, their existence overlooked by her earlier, possibly because they were lost in the confused pattern of the wallpaper. The paintings were of scenes captured in soft tones—rural rivers, trees and mountains. Pretty in their own way.

'Now I see them. They're pretty. My mummy used to paint, and she was teaching me how to. Maybe you can teach me.'

'I doubt it child. You'll be too messy. But that other woman here—Alice—isn't that her name? I'm sure she'll take you under her wing, and maybe with time you might be able to show us something you have done. No messy scribbles mind you. Papa will not tolerate that.'

Deedee nodded and promised to do her best.

'Now off you go. Children should not be allowed into the parlour. In my day this would never have happened. I do not want to see you again unless an adult brings you into the room. Do you understand?'

Deedee nodded again and turned for the door. As she left the room, followed by her aunt, she could still hear the old ladies talking.

'That was a bit harsh sister,' she heard the woman named Cicely say. 'With a wash and some decent attire befitting a young lady, she might be rather pretty.'

'That remains to be seen. But mark my words, I have my doubts.'

'Aunt,' asked Deedee reaching for her aunt's hand as they headed down the corridor towards the kitchen. 'Who were those ladies and why were they so fuzzy? I couldn't have dreamed about them as you also saw them. Unless you were also in my dream. I don't understand.'

'It's a bit much to take in on your first night here. I shouldn't have been surprised you saw them. You are family after all. Most strangers don't see them. All they notice is the sudden coldness in the room when those two wish them gone.'

'But who are they?'

'We're pretty sure they both lived here a long time ago. I've done a bit of sleuthing—you know, checked with the previous owners, and did some research at the local history museum. As far as I can determine, Aunt Eloise is the older sister—a few years older than Aunt Cicely. They both died a long time ago—in the early 1920s— from the Spanish flu I understand, and within a few weeks of each other. A tragedy for the family. With their deaths, there was only one surviving child. Another child had died in early childhood quite a few years before that, but I am not sure from what. I mean children died all the time in those days. But the aunts, that was a tragedy. Young women and I seem to recall one might have lost her fiancé in the First World War. So much sorrow in those days. That might explain why they are sometimes less than welcoming. Just try and be polite to them if they do appear before you. They mean no harm—to family that is. It's strangers they have no time for!'

Pulling her great niece close she continued, 'I think that is more than enough for you to take in today. Let's get you to bed. Too late for a wash and in any event, Eloise and Cicely aren't nearby, so they can't object. A quick wipe of your face and hands with a flannel and the rest will keep until morning. Come this way.'

Deedee followed her aunt back towards the side door and then up a steep set of stairs. The stairs were built from a honey-coloured sort of wood, each tread worn into a dip from the passage of countless feet over the years. Deedee's little feet fitted neatly into the worn slope as if it was always intended that she would walk this way, and for some reason that gave her comfort. At the top of the stairs was a landing containing two open doors.

'This is our bedroom,' Minnie said, pointing to the right. 'And your room is there to the left. We are not far away if you need us in the night. No bathroom up here I'm afraid. If you are caught out, you can either go down the stairs to the bathroom, or you will find a chamber pot under the bed for emergencies. It can be emptied in the morning. Come on Miss, let's get you sorted. Your bed awaits.'

Deedee submitted to a cursory wiping by her great-aunt with a dampened face towel. All this focus on cleanliness was new to her. Her parents' haphazard approach to hygiene was all that she had ever known, but she supposed she would get used to this new regime. In between sweeping wipes by the wet face towel, and the occasional scrub of a recalcitrant spot, Deedee perused her new bedroom. Sloping ceilings indicated that this was an attic room built just under the roofline. A padded window seat by a dormer window seemed the perfect place to linger with a book. An elegantly carved four poster wooden bed, in the same honey tones as the stairs, was piled high with a mass of bedding—more pillows than a little girl could ever need and two fluffy quilts, one folded neatly at the foot of the bed. Deedee's teddy bear had already been transported into the room and lay, neatly placed, on the bed waiting for her appearance. Her aunt reached under the bed and pulled out a round china bowl patterned with blue flowers and leaves.

'Here you go. This is the chamber pot. Just sit on it if you need to do a wee in the night. Or you can go downstairs to the bathroom if you would prefer. I'll leave the stair light on for you. I haven't unpacked all your stuff I'm afraid. We'll worry about doing that tomorrow. But I did find your nightie. Put that on and I'll be back in a few moments to tuck you in. Are you OK?'

Deedee nodded. Strange though this house and its inhabitants were, she thought she might just be okay after all.

Chapter Five

Twenty Years Ago

It sure says a lot about the resilience of youth, Deedee quickly became accustomed to her new life with two women she had no memory of ever meeting, and whose word she had to accept that they were in fact her family. Up until now she had been living in some kind of bubble encapsulated by her father and mother. School friends were meant for the daylight hours during term time. Her friendship with them didn't extend to after school hours except for the times when she was invited to the occasional birthday party. Deedee's universe was her home and her parents. Her father was tall and handsome, with sooty black curly hair; her mother, the epitome of softness and laughter—a lap to climb onto and loving arms to hold her close.

In later years, she would struggle to recall the features of her parents. As all photos were lost in that terrible fire, Deedee had to trust and accept that her great-aunt's descriptions were accurate. That, as an adult, she was a copy of her mother but with different colouring—having inherited the olive skin and shiny dark curls from her father. With her skin and dark hair, and her mother's delicate features, Deedee had a face that was so different from all the other children in this rural town.

Being so different was never an issue in cosmopolitan Sydney, but she was soon to learn that in a small community, standing out from the crowd could be a problem.

At first, Deedee was not aware of how different she was. For the first few days Minnie and Alice kept her close. If they weren't nearby, the black cat would appear making it noticeably clear that he intended to stick by her side. In a way, Deedee found his presence a comfort as she was still not sure of her place in this household. After the first evening, she had stayed away from the front room and those dragon ladies—her instincts telling her that as they were spirits of people long gone, they would be best avoided.

All too soon it was time to go to school. With much fuss, a uniform, hat, shoes, and bag had been purchased along with what was deemed to be essential stationery. Then, one morning in early October, Minnie took her by the hand and escorted her out of the garden—by way of the front gate this time—onto a dusty path that ran alongside the river. They went over the bridge and up a small rise until they reached the local public school. The first morning they arrived, the school bell had not yet been rung. The schoolyard was full of children running, jumping, yelling, and paying no attention to the middle-aged woman and clinging child standing by the gate. An officious looking woman clutching a hand bell and a notepad, bustled towards them. It was clear she meant business.

'Good morning. You must be Deirdre.' It wasn't a question but rather a statement, delivered in an emphatic tone as she fixed a steely gaze on the child. Deedee, dumbstruck, did not reply. It was left up to Minnie to respond.

'Yes, this is my great niece. She may have been baptised Deirdre, but we tend to call her Deedee.'

'We get lots of family names here and to me, they just cause confusion. It will be a matter for her teacher to decide which name she chooses to use. You got here in the nick of time.' These words were delivered with an unspoken message that next time they should endeavour to arrive at the school earlier.

'I'm just about to ring the bell. Then I will show you where to line up with the other Year 3 children. Come this way now. Say goodbye to your aunt.'

With one anguished glance back towards Minnie, Deedee

allowed herself to be led away into the middle of the quadrangle. Minnie raised her hand in farewell then slowly let it fall as Deedee disappeared into the mass of children that swirled around the yard.

That first day at school passed slowly, in a chaos of noise and confusion. Strange children, unfamiliar processes, and an unfamiliar environment—it all conspired to make Deedee feel like she was trapped in a nightmare. The teacher, Miss Smith, did her best to be welcoming. She was young, pretty and fragrant, smelling softly sweet—a bit like apple blossom Deedee thought. She sat Deedee down at the front of the class with another new student who appeared to be equally lost. The other children in the class—noisy and boisterous—monopolised their teacher's attention. So much so that it wasn't until just before the morning recess that she realised she had done little more than seat the two new students.

'Goodness me. You two have been so quiet. As quiet as mice.'

In response to the sniggers now erupting from the fellow classmates, the teacher continued, 'That's quite enough class. Now I want you all to welcome Deirdre and Anita into the class. It's their first day and everything is new, so I expect all of you to be kind and look after them. I need someone to be their buddy ... let me see.' She paused and surveyed the classroom, considering the students who had all suddenly gone silent and, without exception, were looking down in earnest consideration of their desks. 'Yes Libby. You and Emma will do. At break, would you both please look after Deirdre and Anita? Give them a guided tour of the school grounds, show them where the toilets are, and the tuck shop, and anything else you think might be important. I'm relying on you both to be the best buddies ever and I am sure you won't disappoint me.'

Deedee, watching the expressions on the faces of the two girls, was not convinced that Miss Smith's selection was going to be successful. The girl who she now understood to be called Libby, reminded her of a girl appearing in a lead role in certain TV shows she had watched about school, pony club or the like. Those girls who were almost generic in their looks with their long blonde hair, blue eyes, and cute, innocent appearance—and knew it. These girls would be Queen B of the gang and would be the ones who would get their own way in all situations. The other girl, the one known as Emma, was clearly a follower, so evident from the way she looked at Libby for direction. At least Deedee hadn't been left alone to deal with these two—she had the other new student, Anita, who surely would be a support as they settled into the routine of everyday school life. One sideways glance at her companion confirmed Deedee's worst fears. Anita would be no support. In fact, it looked like Deedee would be the one to take care of her and by the look of it, she would always have to have a handkerchief on hand to mop up the tears. With a shrug, she reached into her pocket, located her clean hankie, and passed it to her sniffing neighbour.

Recess was as bad as she had expected.

'Come on mice,' Queen B said as she strutted past their desk. 'This way. I'll only show you once, as I have much more important things to do. So, pay attention. 'Here's the bathroom,' she said while waving her hand to the right towards a detached building across the quadrangle— with separate, marked doors for boys and girls.

'Over there is the canteen. Lunch orders must be written on the brown paper bags and left in the basket by the classroom front door. And if you don't have the right money, don't expect to get any change. This is our school yard but don't go down the back near the trees. That belongs to the Year 6's and they'll beat you up. And no one will rescue you. Me, I can go down there because I'm special and my brother is in Year 6 but ...' She paused, and with a highly effective glare at the two cowering girls, she continued, '... I will not rescue you—ever!'

Libby glanced at her acolyte, Emma, and with a shrug concluded her address.

'That's it from me. You've had your introduction and if our teacher asks how it went, I expect you both to say the right thing. Understood?'

The two 'mice' nodded their heads vigorously and watched the two so-called buddies saunter off without even a backward glance.

'That went well ... didn't it?' Anita said anxiously.

'Not really,' Deedee replied. 'I guess we are on our own and it's pretty clear they are to be avoided. There must be someone nice here.'

With that they both looked around hopefully. Two small children standing alone and apart in a playground, ignored by their fellow students.

Little changed as the school day progressed. The other children acted as if the two newcomers were invisible. It may have been that peer groups had already been established, and there was no perceived need to expand them to include these two others. At least Deedee had the satisfaction of discovering that the schoolwork was easy. The school readers the other children struggled with were an absolute treat for her. The spelling test and mathematics problems presented no challenge at all and best of all, the afternoon ended with a painting class. Their task – to paint a special picture for their mothers, or as Miss Smith said, with a watchful eye on Deedee, 'Whomever it is that is special in your life. It may be a mother, an aunt or a grandmother.'

By the time the bell rang to mark the end of the school day, Deedee had decided there was very little to like about this new school. The teacher might be OK. Her desk companion, Anita, could possibly become a friend ... in time—if only she would stop crying. But the others, well it remained to be seen. At least she could walk home from this school, unlike her old school, which was so far from home that she had to wait until one of her parents arrived to collect her. Today she would have given anything to see one or both of her parents waiting at the school gate. But they weren't, and they never would be. With that in mind, and with her school bag hung haphazardly over one shoulder, she followed the procession of students out the school gate and ran as fast as her little legs could carry her down the hill in the direction of the river and the comfort of her new home.

Crossing the bridge at the river she slowed, paused, and looked down. The murky, brownish water flowed sluggishly under the bridge, caught at the edges by reeds and overhanging willows. Ducks busily worked the edges, diving and resurfacing as they sought out their dinner.

Across the bridge, Deedee turned right and meandered along the path that edged the river. Her aunt had told her that from time to time, the river would flood when there had been a very wet winter. Such floods, she assured her, never threatened their cottage but had been known to cover the river path she now followed, once even lapping at the gate into the garden. As she stopped at the gate to force it open, Deedee tried to imagine a flood that would come so high. At least she thought, if there ever was a flood, maybe she would not be able to get to school.

Leaving her bag by the steps to the front verandah, she followed the path that curved around the garden's boundary until she stopped by a large elm not far from the front gate. With a sigh she sat down, making herself comfortable in a dip that seemed just made for sitting. She wriggled her bottom into the depression and leaned back, resting against the roughened bark of the tree. Never had she felt so alone. As if to emphasise her solitude, the garden fell silent. Birds ceased their scurrying and song and as if holding their breaths, waiting for what would happen next.

Deedee, wrapped up in her misery, paid no attention. All she wanted was for life to return to how it used to be. She was young—only nine years old after all—and all she wanted was her mum—or her dad—either would do.

She wrapped her arms around her knees, rested her chin on them and stared forward, eyes misted by tears. She felt so alone.

There was a rustling behind her, and a whisper—a whisper that was repeated over and over because Deedee, completely consumed by her sadness, was totally unaware of any other noises.

'Psst. Psst. You there. What is wrong?'

This last question penetrated Deedee's misery and she turned to look towards the source of the sound. It wasn't behind her as all that was there was the trunk of the sheltering tree. It was to her left, towards a mass of shrubby bushes. They rustled but there was no wind. That sound again.

'Over here. See? Here I am.'

With that a scruffy head appeared out from behind the bushes, closely followed by the rest of the small boy. Deedee considered his approach. She had never seen him before. He certainly wasn't at school today. And he wasn't dressed in a school uniform. His attire was not far removed from the status of rags. He wore a worn button-up shirt—clearly having undergone some mending—of an indeterminate colour, possibly once a pale blue. His trousers, secured around the waist with string, were ripped and frayed. They were clearly of a great age—maybe hand-me-downs? The boy's face was as grubby as his shirt, and he had a mop of sandy coloured hair that appeared to have been styled with the assistance of a pudding basin.

'Do I know you? Who are you? Why are you here?' Deedee asked, her tears now forgotten.

'I'm here because I could hear you blubbering. You were making such a racket.'

'I do not blubber.' Deedee felt indignant. A quiet cry in the privacy of one's own garden was surely perfectly permissible.

'Sounded like blubbering to me. You frightened away the birds, so I thought I should check that you weren't hurt or something.'

'Oh.' Deedee was taken aback by his concern and didn't know what to say.

The boy sat down beside her, pulled out a knife and a lump of wood, and commenced to whittle, all the while whistling a tune of sorts.

Deedee couldn't help but be fascinated as she watched his fingers move so quickly to shape the wood. Then she remembered her manners.

'My name is Deedee and I live here.'

'You do? Can't say I've ever seen you here before.'

'Well, I really do live here. With my Great-Aunt Minnie and her friend Alice.'

'No need to get all huffy on me. I believe you. It's just I haven't see you here before.'

'Well, why are you here? It's not like this is your home. Who are you?'

'Actually, it is. My home that is. I'm Bertie and this is where I live,' he said while giving a circle of his head to indicate the garden that surrounded them.

'Here?' Deedee felt like she was missing something. Surely the boy couldn't live in the garden, although that might explain his scruffy, unwashed appearance.

'Yes, here,' he said with emphasis as if Deedee was an idiot for not believing him.

'Never mind that for now. Here, take this.' He handed her a small carving, now complete. Deedee turned it over in her hand, examining it in closely. The carving was of a small bird, simply done. Its essence was captured with a few curves that hinted at a rounded body, a small head, and a beak; and a wing created by the indent in the curve. Deedee was amazed.

'Thank you, Bertie. This is so beautiful. Is this for me?'

'Of course. That's why I gave it to you. To cheer you up. Has it worked?'

'Oh yes.' Deedee's smile confirmed her words. Before she could continue, she heard Minnie calling.

'Drat! That's my aunt. I have to go. She's probably been expecting me to be home before this.' For some reason Deedee was reluctant to leave her first real friend in this strange new place.

'Will I see you again Bertie?'

'Too right you will. You can always find me here by this tree. As I said, I live here.'

Deedee, with her head cocked to one side, considered what he had said, but before she could ask anything further, her aunt called again, this time the anxiety clearly obvious in her voice.

Deedee jumped to her feet, carved bird clutched tightly in one hand. With the other hand, she waved goodbye and ran down the path towards the house, her tears now completely forgotten.

Chapter Six

Present Day

In the grey light of pre-dawn, she awoke with a start. The typical comforting night-time sounds were strangely absent. Unable to hear the surge of waves that was usually her evening lullaby, Deedee felt dislocated and uneasy. Then, with increased consciousness came the realisation that she had returned to her childhood environment. No wash and flow of waves here, just a hesitant chirp as birds in the garden cleared their throats in preparation for the dawn chorus. With that awareness, she relaxed back into the mattress. Of course, she was back home warm and comfortable in her four-poster bed, surrounded by all those treasures that had been collected throughout her childhood. With a sigh, she turned over and went back to sleep—that morning's avian performance unheard and unappreciated by the young woman at rest, her soft snoring creating a performance all of its own.

It wasn't until several hours later that a freshly washed and dressed Deedee wandered into the kitchen looking for some breakfast. Her aunt, up and about long ago—or as much as she could currently manage—was making a pot of tea in the kitchen.

'Good morning. Just in time Deedee dear. I have put some bread on to toast and am just making a pot of tea. I thought we might sit in the sunroom and have our breakfast there. But only if you carry the tray for me that is. I think it might be a bit too much for me. But I could manage carrying the plates for us.'

'Sounds perfect Aunt. Tea and toast overlooking the garden – great idea. And now that you mention food, I find I'm starving,' said Deedee, her stomach giving an anticipatory gurgle.

'And you hinted *I* was underfed. Sounds like your tummy is of the same opinion about you!'

They settled into the white cane chairs clustered around the table in a glass enclosed sunroom overlooking the garden and only a short distance from the kitchen. Minnie busied herself spreading a thick covering of butter on her toast before adding generous spoonfuls of jam—homemade blackberry jam by the looks of it.

'Ah,' she sighed after having taken one bite, and chewing and swallowing with relish. 'I must say, this is excellent jam. Made by myself of course,' Minnie added not so modestly. 'And this is the perfect place to sit. It's warm and sunny, and a good spot to look out for that dratted boy.'

'What boy?'

For a moment, some fragmentary memories resurfaced in her mind. Memories of her as a child running along these garden paths chasing a boy. But what boy? And surely, he would be grown up by now?

'What boy?' she repeated, her question remaining unanswered. Maybe her aunt was going deaf?

'You know. That boy that helps me in the garden. The one who has been keeping an eye on things while I was in hospital. Now what was his name?'

As Minnie shook her head in annoyance, it became clear to Deedee who she meant.

'You mean Harry. Harry Frost. Is he meant to be visiting today?'

'He will be if he wants to be paid. Mind you, I see no need to get any work done but Harry tells me the place is so overgrown it has become a fire hazard. I suppose he is right,' Minnie grudgingly conceded. 'It has been a lot to manage on my own. Once, when Alice was still alive, we would work out in the garden together. Most afternoons after she had completed her painting for the day, you would find us outside clipping and weeding, and sometimes just sitting.' Minnie, remembering those times not that long ago, smiled and turned to face Deedee, a fierce look in her eyes.

'I miss her you know. She really was my better half. Made the world a brighter place for me.'

Deedee leaned towards her aunt and took one of her skeletal hands, holding it gently between hers.

'I know,' she said patting her aunt's hand. 'I miss her too. There's not much I remember about my time before I moved here—just fragments really. But I do know that you and Alice were the making of me. You both turned your lives upside down and made me a home—a loving home—and I will be forever grateful. I also wish Alice was still here with us, in part so I could show her my latest work.'

'Hmmph,' Minnie said in response. 'I'm not so sure you really mean that. Think about it. Do you think Alice would approve of your current occupation as an illustrator? I'm positive she wouldn't. She believed in your talent and thought you would end up a better artist than she ever was.'

Minnie looked fiercely at her niece as if urging her to disagree. The underlying message that she had somehow disappointed her beloved aunts was not lost on Deedee. Sometimes when she worked on yet another book of quaint illustrations, she wondered the same thing. Still, it was one thing to consider such matters yourself and quite another to be lectured by a relative, no matter how beloved that relative was.

'Possibly,' she replied. That was as much as she was prepared to admit for now.

'Definitely,' came the immediate response. 'But never mind. All that can be changed now that you are here. I'll get that dratted boy, once he arrives, to make a start on clearing the path to Alice's studio and you can set it up for your own use. All her stuff is still there. I didn't have the heart to move it and as you may recall, the light in the studio is excellent. You should know. You were always there as a little one, getting under Alice's feet and into her paints. She had the patience of a saint that woman.'

Deedee was at a loss as to how to respond and explain to her aunt that her stay was not intended to be a long one. It was becoming increasingly clear that her aunt, now that she had become accustomed to Deedee's visit, considered her great niece had returned home permanently. Deedee could feel herself resenting what she considered to be Minnie's railroading of her future. After all, she had a perfectly good life in Sydney. She had a career that provided a satisfactory income—even though she silently agreed that it might not always be artistically satisfying, a home by the sea that soothed her soul, and enough friends that meant she only needed to be alone when she chose to be. However, with one glance at her aunt's anxious face, Deedee realised that this was not the time to be sharing these thoughts with Minnie, as she may have been speaking from a place of loneliness and a wish for company. Glancing past her aunt and out the window, Deedee noticed movement along the path— it was the now familiar shape of Harry Frost. Clad once again in his horticultural uniform, he strode towards the side door, this time accompanied by a dog of strange appearance—it was medium sized and scruffy, with a shaggy coat of cream and tan.

'Aunt, I think Harry is here. And with a dog!'

'About time! Just because I'm old and retired that boy thinks he can turn up any time he likes,' Minnie said with a twinkle in her eye. Deedee somehow thought her aunt might be rather fond of Harry.

'And the dog? Won't Merlin object?'

'Not at all. That dog has met Merlin many times and knows his place. He usually sits here in the sunroom with me, always on the lookout for treats. Don't you mind Scruff. Merlin certainly doesn't.'

Harry knocked on the door, shouted 'hello' and entered the house. He wandered down the corridor towards the sunroom, his face beaming as he entered. He was followed by a scampering dog bouncing his way towards Minnie as if he was greeting a long-lost friend.

'Finally. You're here at last. Down you dratted dog,' Minnie said while pushing a jubilant Scruff onto all four legs. 'Harry, do you remember my niece Deedee?'

Harry grinned across at Deedee, laughter twinkling in his amazing eyes. They were the colour of the bushes he so often tended—green with a touch of dirt.

'Of course. How could I forget young Deedee from school? And we got reacquainted the other day, just before you returned from hospital. I popped in to feed Merlin and found her already here. Great to see you again Deedee,' he added. 'Have you got Minnie all sorted out yet?'

'More like she's got me sorted out!'

Harry smiled. 'Nothing changes around here. As far as our Minnie is concerned, you'll always be her little girl and I'll always be young Harry, or that dratted boy. Am I right?'

Deedee couldn't help but laugh. Harry had nailed it! They smiled at each other in a friendly collusion against Minnie. And that wasn't a situation Minnie could tolerate. After all, she was the one that should always be the centre of attention.

'Never mind that you two. Enough chummy chummy behaviour and meaningful glances. It's time you did some work young Harry, or you won't get paid. Now, I want you to clear that path up to Alice's studio first thing, so Deedee can get up there. Then you can attack all those parts of the garden you are nagging me about. Deedee can help you. It'll be good for you dear, to get outside in the sunshine. Off you both go.' And with a regal wave like a presiding member of royalty, Deedee and Harry found they were dismissed. Scruff remained by Minnie's side, distracted by the treats graciously being offered to him.

'Is she always like this?' Deedee asked as they moved through the side gate to collect Harry's gardening tools from his utility.

'Pretty much. She's got no one else to boss around anymore, you see. Anyway, her bark is worse than her bite. I think she is lonely. When she gets too annoying, I try to remember how kind she and Alice were to me when I was little. She encouraged me to set up this business on my own, you know. And she was my first customer. I owe her a lot. So, if she wants to be a bit bossy from time to time, I can cope. And Scruff likes her. You know what they say, animals are a good judge of character—better than humans I suspect. Here take this,' he said handing Deedee a pair of secateurs. 'You can trim some of the overgrowth. Put it in this big bag and I'll tackle the other stuff.'

The crazy paved stone path to Alice's studio wound its way from out the side of the house, around the back, and up a slight slope. It was on that slope that the undergrowth had taken off in the months following Alice's short illness and death.

With care, Deedee cut the roses that bordered the path. A late pruning, she acknowledged. Now that spring was well established, this should have been done months ago when the bushes were in winter dormancy. She could already see the new leafy growth swelling and bursting from the stalks. She contented herself with trimming only those branches that overhung the path and threatened any passers-by with their thorns. A further trim once the roses had finished their first flowering would be enough, she thought.

'You know my family owned this house once?' Harry said as he dug around a wayward sapling soon to be removed from its home.

'No. I didn't. When?'

'Ages ago. Minnie bought it from my grandpa when she first arrived here—before Alice came on the scene. Grandpa had to sell up so he could move in with us and help Mum when Dad got ill. It suited him to sell to Minnie. I think he saw it as passing the house onto someone who would care for it. Although, he would still come back from time to time and just sit on the front porch. He used to say he was catching up with his ancestors. Said his people had built the house, his father had been born in the front room and so had he. He had lots of stories about the place. Some happy and some sad.'

'Did you spend much time here when you were little?'

'I suppose I did when I was young, while Grandpa still lived here. But to be honest, I don't remember much apart from always feeling safe. I just loved being in this garden.'

Harry stood to his full height, stretched and looked around.

'Guess I still do. That's why I'm happy to give Minnie a hand any time she needs me.'

Deedee paused mid cut, secateurs stilling as she considered what Harry had just said. So many of her childhood memories were a maze of confusion—a muddle of events and people. Sometimes it seemed to her that her real life only commenced when she started art school as a young adult. Perhaps that was because she had pushed the earlier memories away. Perhaps. But in that muddle of memories were vague recollections of a young Deedee playing in this garden—chasing someone or being chased around the circuitous paths that meandered throughout the yard. Although she couldn't recall the identity of her playmate, she could still recall the feelings of happiness and companionship that she shared with this mystery friend. Could it have been Harry? For some reason, she needed to know.

'Harry, did you ever visit here when I was a child and play in this garden with me?' she asked in a wondering tone.

'Nah. I was a bit older than you—about three years ahead of you at school. No offence Deedee, but you were a bit too young to be a friend at school. Anyway, I was into sport—cricket, footie and tennis—but I knew who you were and on occasion looked out for you. I don't know if you remember too much about your childhood here, but that school we attended could be rather rough. In those early days ... well, you were a bit out of your depth being a city girl and all.'

Harry put down his shovel, moved towards a nearby wooden bench, and gestured for Deedee to join him. He reached into his backpack and produced thermos, mugs and what looked like cake wrapped tightly in foil. Deedee had no hesitation in following him. Gardening was such hungry work, and she was eager to continue this conversation.

Harry busied himself pouring what appeared to be coffee into two tin mugs and handed one to Deedee.

'No milk I'm afraid. But it is good coffee. I brewed it myself. You can always get some milk from inside if you want.'

'No, I'm fine. And thank you, I will try some of your cake. Made this yourself too?'

'Not likely. My cooking skills are abysmal. Thank Mum. She does a mean fruit cake.'

For a moment, all was silent as they both sipped and chewed. Then Deedee returned to their earlier conversation.

'What did you mean when you said school was rough and I was out of my depth?'

'Only in the early days. Mind you, I wasn't around for more than your first year there anyway, and I think by the time I left for high school, you had toughened up. I remember first seeing you in Year 3. I was in Year 6 then. You know, I was the big fish in a small pond—school captain and all that—so I suppose I felt I had to look after the little ones, the waifs and strays so to speak.'

'Waifs and strays? Me?' Deedee's indignation was clearly apparent.

'Yep. Too right. But as I said, not for long. I saved you once you know. Saved you from that dreaded Libby. My, she was a right bitch. She still is really, and I should know—I went out with her for a few years until I came to my senses. But that's another story. My grandpa used to say that most people couldn't, or wouldn't, change. He reckoned badness could be in the bones and would be with a person—or an animal for that matter—for life. I don't know if he is right, but that Libby—well, she was a cow at school and is still a piece of work. She gets away with it though, cause she's a looker and can lay on the charm when she wants something. Believe me, I know.'

Harry's monologue drifted over Deedee as she struggled to recall those days from so long ago. Certainly, she remembered feelings of misery when she first came to live with Minnie and Alice. But surely that was understandable. Her parents and her entire world had disappeared completely in just one evening. All that was familiar was gone and she had to learn to quickly adapt to a strange environment. Surely anyone in those circumstances would be miserable, and it was only to be expected that it would take time to recover. But had there been something or someone else also making her miserable?

'You saved me? How?'

'Well, it was a while back and I can't say the memory is all that clear now that I think about it, but I seem to recall that I came across you being bullied by Libby one afternoon after school. Was she in the same class as you?

Seeing Deedee's tentative nod, he continued.

'Yeah, that would be it. She was probably jealous of you—seeing you as competition. The new girl at school surrounded by an aura of tragedy. You must admit, your circumstances at the time were awfully tragic. None of it was your fault of course and on top of that you were different. In this Anglo town of blonde or red hair, and blue eyes, you stood out like the proverbial tits on a bull. Black hair, olive skin and your dark eyes—almost as black as coal. You clearly weren't someone from around here. People don't like things or people that are different—it's a herd thing I suppose. Not something that should be encouraged, but there you go. It happens, and we should always try to fight against it. As I did when I gave Libby what for.'

Harry took Deedee's now empty mug and peered intently into her eyes.

'Remember any of this, do you?'

She shook her head.

'Not really. Just memories of feeling miserable and friendless.'

Chapter Seven

Twenty Years Ago

The first week at this strange new school was now behind her. Deedee told herself that things should now be feeling more familiar, yet somehow so much still felt strange. Not everything perhaps. The walk to school was known, as was the routine followed each morning: the school bell rung promptly at 9:00 am whereupon all the children would gather in the quadrangle, falling into a line for each class. As Deedee now knew to which line she belonged, she would stand quietly to listen to whatever wisdom the headmistress imparted to the gathering before each class walked away—still in line following their teacher—like so many ducklings following Mother Duck.

Lessons were not too bad. They were pretty much like the lessons at her last school, and some were even fun, like reading and art. Some were to be endured—especially maths—and some were new to her—such as the time spent in the school garden each afternoon after lunch. It was only half an hour, but Deedee found it strangely interesting. One such afternoon, Deedee and Anita were tasked with planting lettuce seedlings under Miss Smith's supervision. Carefully, being mindful of the fragility of these baby plants, they worked to ease the seedlings apart and then, with grubby fingers, they bedded them into the soil that had already been prepared by the other students. Two of the boys in the class gave them a quick water using the hose, but for some reason they watered more than just the lettuce seedlings. Even though she had become rather damp, Deedee thought that the gardening lesson could very well turn into her favourite class, or at the very least slot in alongside her other favourite—art.

That afternoon, the school bell having been rung to mark the end of the day, the children in Deedee's class rushed to their bags hung on hooks outside the classroom. Carefully, because she was that sort of child, Deedee took her bag off the hook, put her homework and pencil case inside, then hoisting her backpack over one shoulder, she headed down the verandah steps in the direction of the path home.

Crossing the quadrangle, she was lost in her own thoughts and paid no attention to the chatter of the other children. Until, with a thud, she was jerked back to reality. A thud as another body collided with hers, pushing her to the ground and sending her backpack flying. With the breath knocked out of her, Deedee shuddered with the effort to inhale. The suddenness of the assault so unexpected that her first reaction was a feeling of shock and not tears. She could see her backpack lying on one side, papers scattered and pencils spilling out of her now shattered pencil case.

A foot, in regulation white socks and a polished black shoe, negligently stirred the papers before stepping on them, leaving a dirty mark. A voice dripping with insincerity pierced Deedee's consciousness.

'How sad. Poor little mouse. You tripped and fell and were so careless with your schoolwork. I don't know what Miss Smith will say on Monday when she sees the mess you have made with your homework.'

As if to emphasise the point, she slowly moved her foot in a circle in an effort to scrunch the papers. Her homework was now not only dirty, but it was a mess. Moving towards her scattered possessions, Deedee applied herself first to the task of collecting her pencils. This she could do away from the voice that just kept droning on. From the corner of her eye, she could see the other children leaving the quadrangle, leaving her and her torturer alone. The voice continued with its hurtful patter.

'Such a pathetic little mouse. All alone and no one to help you. Here let me.' With that she bent over and collected the now scrunched papers. Using both hands she crumpled them further into a tight ball and pushed them into Deedee's backpack.

'There, that should do it. Now you can scurry back to the little mouse hole where you live with those nasty old witchy ladies. You don't belong here, do you understand? I don't want your grubby little mouse-like body anywhere near me. I hope that has got through your thick little black-haired head.'

Tears obscured Deedee's vision. The venom of this attack and the hatred she spat out with every syllable was beyond anything she had encountered in her short life. She had no ammunition to ward off such an enemy. All she could do was put her head down, avoid eye contact and focus on repacking her bag. Would the attack cease, or would this person continue with the physical and verbal abuse? Could she run fast enough to get down the hill to the safety of her home to get away from the current threat? Then, without warning, the situation changed. Deedee's rescuer—not a knight on a white charger, but a scruffy Year 6 boy wandering casually across the quadrangle, idly swinging a tennis racquet in his hand.

'Hiya Libby. What's happening?'

Deedee's heart plummeted to her stomach. This boy seemed to know Libby, and this could only signify that worse was yet to come. Deedee tensed and prepared herself for further onslaught. Maybe if they were distracted, she could make a run for it. Even if it meant leaving her bag behind, at least she could get a head start and bolt for the safety of home.

'Harry. Hi.'

Libby's tone changed. No longer hectoring, she spoke in a sweet, simpering voice. She could almost have been a different person and maybe with this new audience, she was. But Harry was not fooled.

'I saw what you did. I won't report you this time, but you know that I can. I'm school captain after all,' he said puffing his chest out and pointing to the shiny badge pinned on his chest. 'But I'll only not report you if you do two things—one now, and one later on.'

The tears started to flow. But this time the tears were from Libby and not Deedee.

'Harry. It's a misunderstanding, that's all. I meant no harm.'

'Yeah right. Not only did I see what you did, but I also heard what you said. As did half the school, and they've no doubt run home to blab on you.' His voice became stern. 'First thing you will do is swap your homework sheets with Deedee's. That way she will have the clean set and you can work out what sort of excuse you can give next week for your messy set. But no blaming anyone but yourself, do ya hear?'

Harry tapped his racquet with one hand, all the while watching Libby. They locked eyes and gazed at each other, neither of them willing to give any ground.

'I'm waiting,' Harry said. He glanced past the girls as he continued. 'Hello Miss Smith.'

'Is everything okay here Harry?'

'Yes, Miss Smith. I'm just going to walk Deedee home. It is her first week here after all and I thought she might like the company. Libby was going to walk with her as well, but she's just remembered she has to be somewhere else.'

'Thank you, Harry and Libby. I really appreciate how you are looking after Deedee. I'm sure she is grateful to have such good friends as you two. I'll keep going then and see you all bright and early on Monday. Have a lovely weekend then, won't you?'

To a chorus of, 'Thank you Miss Smith' and 'Bye Miss Smith,' she wandered away leaving the three children facing each other.

'I'm still waiting Libby. I didn't blab then because I'm sure you will do the right thing. So, don't disappoint me. Get moving and swap the homework papers ... now!' The hand tapping the tennis racquet increased in intensity.

Knowing she was licked; Libby did the deed. She pulled the scrunched-up mess out of Deedee's bag and replaced them with her own pristine homework sheets. Deedee focused on collecting the last of her pencils, avoided looking at Libby. Not that Libby would have noticed as all her attention was on Harry.

'I didn't mean it, you know. She's just a pain. She deserves it. Who does she think she is moving here where she's not wanted?' Libby whined.

'That's quite enough Libby.' Harry sounded almost parental in his scorn. 'Leave Deedee alone. In fact, that's exactly the second thing you will do. Leave her alone. You don't need to be friends and you can ignore her if that suits you best. But no more bullying. No more nasty words or shoves. No more calling her 'mouse'. That's not her name, just as I won't call you 'bully'. But I'll be watching, don't ever forget that. And I have my spies!'

Turning to Deedee, he took her bag in his spare hand.

'Come on Deedee. Let's get you home. I like your place. You can show me around if you like. It was once my grandpa's home, you know. I can show you a cool place for a cubby in the garden—or maybe you've already found it.'

The sound of their voices, engaged in conversation about the best location for a cubby house, lingered then faded as the two young children wandered out of the quadrangle, leaving a glowering Libby still clutching the now destroyed homework sheets in her hands. Maybe on Monday she could convince her mother that she was so ill that going to school was not possible?

Chapter Eight

Present Day

'Now I remember. I'd really forgotten all about that. Perhaps I blocked out the misery of those first few weeks. And it was you who rescued me? To be fair, Libby was as good as her word. She never came near me again. Thank you. Although my time at that school had its sad moments, at least it was tolerable. And it's all thanks to you. I'm sure if you hadn't intervened that day, the bullying would have continued.'

'Maybe. Until you learned to punch them out. In my experience, it's the only thing that works with a bully. That or being a bigger bully! Anyway, it looks like you can take care of yourself these days. You're not the little midget you once were. Come on, no more slacking. Back to work!'

A short while later, they both stopped for breath and surveyed the progress they had made. The path to Alice's studio was now exposed and navigable, overhanging branches and rambling roses cut back. The studio, a small weatherboard structure with a bright red front door flanked by a multi-paned glass window, was now revealed to them.

'You're going to need a broom,' Harry said, hands on hips surveying the structure. 'If there are that many cobwebs covering the outside, just imagine how many there'll be inside.'

'So, I take it that your assistance doesn't extend to clearing away scuttling creatures?'

'No way! I'm only a specialist in horticulture, I do not do that other stuff. Anyway, I have heaps more to do elsewhere in the garden. I'll leave you to your dusting! I'll be back later to collect the clippings.' And with a wave, he collected his tools and wandered away, the sound of his tuneless whistle receding and fading into the distance.

'Dusting? As if,' Deedee muttered to herself as she stood before the rustic building. Taking one of the recently trimmed branches in one hand, she swiped it across the door to remove the worst of the cobwebs before doing the same to the small window.

'There, that should do it. At least enough cobwebs removed to let me get in,' she muttered to herself.

With a bit of a shove and a struggle with the handle, the door surrendered and opened with a creak of rusty hinges.

'Mmm, not only do I need to find the broom, but I also need to locate some oil to put on those rusty hinges. What else I wonder?'

With the door now fully open, Deedee entered the room, paused, and looked around. Her nostrils tingled as she inhaled the unique aroma—a distinctive smell of oil paint and turpentine. Just one sniff took her back to her childhood when she would spend countless hours happily working with Alice in this very room. Deedee would work on projects of great importance to her at the time, whether it was the typical finger paintings and potato prints of a nine-year-old, or her later increasingly sophisticated sketches and paintings as her talent matured under Alice's patient guidance.

The studio looked much the same as she recalled it from the last time she had been up, some years before. Some of her earlier paintings remained—unframed and randomly stuck on the walls with thumb tacks. The wall space was shared with some of Alice's preparatory sketches, and various images ripped out of magazines that once may have been appealing or thought to be inspirational.

Along one wall stood two easels containing unfinished paintings which, to Deedee, looked rather forlorn. Alice's paints and paint sticks were scattered in a haphazard mess along a bench that ran along another wall. In the corner stood a comfortable chair covered with a paint-splattered cloth. The room was just how she remembered it. The all-pervading smell of oil paints brought back so many memories—happy and contented memories, so different to her memories from school. This truly had been Deedee's happy place. Countless hours had been spent here, always in the company of Alice, for it was Alice's domain to which she had willingly granted Deedee access.

The reality of using this space without Alice to guide her, hit Deedee full on. How could she even begin to contemplate using this studio without her beloved Aunt Alice beside her? Yet, it was clear that Minnie expected her to do just that. But could she bear to do it when with every glance in any direction brought back painful memories of Alice, reinforcing her feelings of loss.

'Not yet. Not now. Maybe one day.' And with a shake of her head, Deedee backed out of the studio, carefully secured the door, and headed back to the house—to join her living aunt and attend to the chores that awaited her there.

Chapter Nine

Minerva aka 'Minnie'

'Being old is the pits,' Minnie thought as she struggled to her feet and with care in every step, felt her way to the bathroom. It seemed like she had only just got into her bed and already she needed to go to the bathroom. It was years—lifetimes even—since she had been able to make it through the night without needing to go to the toilet.

The aches and pains that now beset her, were only getting worse. Every day a different part of her body complained or jostled for her attention. That young doctor at the hospital gave her no sympathy, spoke of it as being arthritis, implying that it should be accepted as part and parcel of old age. Sometimes, in her dreams, she relived those days when she was young and agile. Running on the beach, dancing at a ball, and enjoying her life with Alice.

Alice—yes Alice. That was the worst part of old age, saying goodbye to the love of her life—waking up bereft every morning, facing each day alone and knowing a vista of many more such empty days stretched out before her. The companionship her and Alice shared for so many years—the love and laughter, and occasional bickering—Minnie had taken for granted. It was only now that it was gone that Minnie realised how much such things had coloured her life and made it worth living. It wasn't even that there had been time for her to prepare for this next stage in her life. The changes had hit her like an avalanche. It seemed like one minute their time together had been full on, filled with shared activity and making plans, then the next—well, those last days of Alice's life just didn't bear thinking about. It was best to remember her as she once was—lurching between excitement or despair about her latest painting. She never did things by halves. Or the two of them working in the garden—shoulder to shoulder—weeding, pruning or planting. All activities were focused on a shared future outcome—flowering in spring, fruiting in summer, or autumn, or whatever. Now, it seemed like some days she was living in a world of black and white, devoid of colour and energy. There no longer seemed any point in doing those things that she had once enjoyed so much. Why bother when no one cared about the end result? There was no Alice to share her activities with. All she had to look forward to now was a continuing sense of loss—that and endless pain—impacting upon her body and her mind.

That boy, that young Harry, might nag her to tidy up the garden, but Minnie found it hard to understand what the point was any more. There was no pleasure to be had in the flowering if she could no longer share it with her beloved. Still, that Harry didn't take no for an answer and had worn her down. To be honest, she had a soft spot for the boy and liked to see his cheerful face. The dog was also good company. He seemed to know that his place was beside her. Maybe the treats did their part, although she liked to think he actually preferred her company. And she quite enjoyed having the dog beside her if only just to annoy the cat.

Back in bed with her doona pulled up tight and close, she contemplated the possibility of sleep. It was most unlikely as the aches in her back and hips swelled in a chorus of complaint. No, they would not let her relax into unconsciousness. All she could do was lie here and contemplate her worries. Her biggest worry—what to do about Deedee. Minnie was well aware that if this question was put to Deedee, she would respond by saying there was no need to do anything and that she could well look after herself.

But one look at her niece, or great-niece to be accurate, and Minnie could see that all was not as it should be in Deedee's world.

Minnie reminded herself that Deedee had always been reserved, keeping so much of what she felt to herself. She supposed the childhood trauma of her parent's tragic death had played its part in the shaping of Deedee's personality. Still, there was something else that didn't feel quite right to Minnie. Not that Minnie was terribly perceptive, but even she could sense a lethargy in the girl. A broken heart perhaps? Or could it be those illustrations for that dreadful book she was working on? Both Minnie and Alice had believed in Deedee's artistic gifts and had done everything they could to foster her talent, even sending her away to a boarding school said to have an amazing arts programme. It was a decision that was initially not welcomed by their niece and it was probably the hardest thing the two women had ever done. They both loved her so.

But they both thought the decision had paid off as Deedee's talent had been fostered and she had flourished. Art school followed and then nothing. Well, not exactly nothing, just not the career path the two aunts had expected. This would be fine, Minnie thought, if she could feel that her girl was happy, but somehow that was not the impression she was getting.

Minnie knew that finding out what was really going on would be so much easier if Alice was still alive. She was a gentler soul and not as abrasive as Minnie. Alice, with her care and compassion, was able to ease the information out of anyone and as a result, she was always a much-loved friend in the community. Minnie could almost hear her whispering in her ear, '*Go on. You can do it. You love our girl just as much as I do. You owe it to her. I'm relying on you to sort out the problem. If not, I might just haunt you!*'

Minnie snorted and spoke out loud. 'I wish! Your company would be so much better than that of the other inhabitants in this draughty old house.'

Somehow the thought of what she needed to do in the coming days eased Minnie's mind, and with a sigh she closed her eyes and drifted off. Like her niece (or great-niece if you want to be picky), the dawn chorus escaped her notice.

Chapter Ten

If she wasn't prepared to work in the old studio at the moment, she could at least sit at the table outside in the garden and continue with her drawing. The day was fine. She could hear the birds chirping and going about their business scratching in the undergrowth. Maybe she should join them and occupy herself with her own activities until such time as Minnie needed something for lunch. A quick glance in the sunroom confirmed there was no need to disturb Minnie. Both her and a certain scruffy dog were unaware of Deedee's existence—Minnie asleep in the sun, dog sprawled at her feet—keeping each other company with their rhythmic snoring.

Retrieving her sketch pad and battered satchel containing her pencils and painting gear from where she left them last night by the fire, Deedee tiptoed outside and headed towards the old elm, under which a table and chair remained. The table, built of solid slabs of timber, had been there for as long as she could remember. It was a relic from times long ago, weathered but still sturdy. Having been the scene of many family celebrations, it bore the scars of people long gone—carved initials, scratches and stains. A few more stains from spilled paints would not matter Deedee thought.

With last night's sketch as a guide, she busied herself with her painting. Soon engrossed, she created a similar image to what she had previously drawn. Deedee knew it would take a while as painting with watercolours could not be rushed. The first sweep of colour to the paper would form the foundation for the scene and give the depth to the background on which, when dry, she would start to create the different shades representing the woodlands where Wendy would find and free the dog from its cage. There wasn't much sky to paint as it would be obscured by trees. But before she could paint those trees, Deedee would need to first paint the watery blue sky that would peep through from between the branches.

As she worked through the process of painting—brush dipped in water, swirled in the watercolour paint of choice, and washed across the page, Deedee's thoughts turned towards her aunt. Somehow, Deedee needed to have a discussion with her about her aunt's future and find out a bit more about what she had been told by the doctors. It was always possible that there may be a medical explanation for her weight loss, or it could be associated with the grief she was undoubtedly still feeling. Either way, she felt it was her responsibility to find out, even if her aunt would object to such a discussion. Minnie had always been a very private person, and Deedee expected any questions from her would be seen as unnecessary prying and an unwarranted intrusion into her aunt's privacy. But did she have an alternative? She was the only living relative as far as she was aware. With a sinking feeling she realised that her own options were also limited. If Minnie needed her niece to move back home to care for her, then she had no choice but to do so. There was no one else that could move in. If only Minnie and Alice had been blessed with a family, there would be someone else with whom she could share this responsibility. But there was no point wishing for something she didn't have. With a sigh, Deedee placed the paintbrush in the glass full of water and contemplated her work to date. Not too bad she thought, now to leave it to dry.

A rustle in the bushes caught her attention. As she glanced towards the sound, Deedee could see the bushes near the elm tree moving as if being blown by a breeze. A few remnants of autumn leaves that lingered under the tree, tumbled across the path. Yet, there was no breeze to be felt. Deedee's painting lay flat and undisturbed on the table. Maybe the movement in the bushes was Merlin, but that still did not explain the tumbling leaves.

'Who's there. Is that you Harry?'

Nothing. But still the bushes continued to shake. Deedee stood and tentatively walked across to the bushes. If the disturbance wasn't being made by Merlin, perhaps it was Harry playing some sort of trick on her. Yet, he didn't really seem like that sort of person—too steady and reliable for high jinks and anyway, she could hear him some distance away in the garden, the sound of his tuneless singing competing with the rasp of a handsaw. So, what was it? Now that she was closer, the bushes slowed their rustle and the nearby birds fell quiet.

'Who is it? Come out and show yourself.'

'No need to make a fuss missus,' came a small voice and with that, a tousle-haired boy emerged from the bushes. He seemed strangely familiar, but Deedee didn't know how this could be.

'Who are you? What are you doing here?'

'I could ask the same of you missus. Do you belong here?'

'Of course, I do. I live here!' Deedee could feel herself becoming flustered. How dare this urchin question her? *He* was the trespasser after all.

'Can't say I've seen you before. Only the old lady and the gardener—Harry, I think. The other old lady—well, she's gone. I thought she might still be here somewhere—in the studio maybe, but no sign of her.' The boy peered intently at Deedee as if she was some insect to be studied under a microscope. 'Are you sure I don't know you? You somehow seem familiar. What is your name?'

'Deedee. What's yours?'

'Bertie. But you know that. I knew you once when you were little. Do you still have my bird?'

The image of a small, hand carved bird sprung to mind. The little bird that had been her constant companion throughout childhood—and adulthood for that matter. Worn to a golden sheen with constant handling and always at rest on top of her bedside table, wherever she lived. The first thing she saw in the morning and the last thing she saw at night. In fact, the first thing she packed the other day when she was getting ready to drive here, and now nesting on top of her bedside table upstairs.

'Yes, I still have the bird. It's so beautiful. How do you know that?'

'I made it for you. Remember?' And with that the small boy looked deeply into Deedee's eyes as if commanding the memories to resurface—and they did.

'Bertie. Of course. You were my friend all those years ago. My only friend to be honest. Forgive me, but somehow you had slipped my mind and I wasn't expecting to see you here.'

He gave a slight shrug as if being forgotten was of no consequence to him.

'It happens. Children remember, but adults rarely do. Though the old lady still sees me, as does her pesky cat. And that gardener sometimes. Especially when I move his tools. He notices that!'

Deedee beckoned and the small boy emerged from under the bushes. She remembered that once they were much the same size. Whereas she had now grown and was an adult of medium height. Bertie, on the other hand, remained the height and size of a small boy. As she contemplated his appearance, she realised that *that* was exactly what had continued to be—a small boy. He was dressed in attire that seemed much like what she recalled he used to wear— frayed grubby trousers held up with string, and a worn, faded blue shirt that was merely hanging on his skinny body by a thread. His mop top was cut in a jagged circle, much like a basin cut, which flew in all directions as he jumped up and down excitedly.

'I knew it! I knew you would come back some day. Do you want to play? Chasings or build a fort?'

The memories came flooding back. This little scruff was indeed her partner in crime from all those years ago. The one who waited for her in the garden every afternoon when she returned sad and dejected from a day of enduring school. The one who made all those miserable thoughts disappear with his wild energy and crazy activities. If only he could still have that effect!

Deedee shook her head.

'Sadly, no. I'm a bit too old and boring for such games, but you can keep me company while I paint and maybe tell me what has been happening here. I'm not much use for you but I do hope we can still be friends.'

'Sure thing missus Deedee. I'll keep you company and watch out for you. It's not safe here you know. Strange people come into the garden from the river way … after dark. They prowl around. I try to frighten them off and sometimes it works, especially when I blow down their necks! One, a man with dark hair like yours, has a notebook. He takes measurements and writes stuff down. If I could, I would make his book disappear, but he keeps tight hold of it. It just doesn't seem right Deedee missus.'

An intruder? Who could it be and why? She didn't want to worry her aunt, but maybe she should ask her if something else was going on. Maybe they should lock the gate. Here she was being concerned about her aunt's health, and now there was another matter to worry about. What else could go wrong? The boy looked at her, his brow wrinkled with concern. It seemed rather bizarre that this spirit child should be worried about her. Surely his worries should be long gone by now. She reached out to him and was not at all surprised when her hand went right through his arm. Definitely a spirit child then, which explained why his appearance had not changed despite the passing of many years since they had last met.

'Don't you worry. With you on guard, no one can get through unnoticed. I'll try and find out what is going on, and hopefully we can reach a solution. After all, this is home to all of us, so whatever is happening is a matter for us all to sort out.' As she said these words, supposedly in comfort of a person long gone, Deedee realised that she was also trying to reassure herself. The thought of her childhood home being under threat from something, or *someone*, unknown was immediately abhorrent to her. Perhaps a place that was once considered her refuge could still be important to her? Or maybe it was the people that belong here that somehow concerned her.

Despite her endeavours to settle the child at the table with her, he showed little interest in lingering. Too soon he wandered off, singing a tuneless song in a soft voice that sounded a bit like the one Harry was singing earlier—and was still singing as he came tramping along the path. There was nothing subtle about Harry and there was no way he could possibly sneak up on her. Deedee looked up and considered his approach. The dirt wiped on the sides of his trousers and down the front of his shirt, the stray leaves caught in his baseball cap, and the broad grin he wore on his face, all told the story of a successful morning taming the garden.

'Sorted it out then?' Deedee asked with an answering smile.

'Enough for now. I thought I might wake up the two slackers inside and see if I can rustle up some coffee and, if I'm lucky, maybe there is something we can have for lunch. Fancy joining me or are you still busy?'

'Not busy at all. I've pretty much done all I can do today. I was just contemplating the garden.'

'Yeah, right.' Harry gave a knowing grin. 'Did our friend disturb you? You're sitting in his part of the garden after all.'

'Our friend?'

'Yeah. Bertie. I can see by your expression you know exactly who I'm talking about. Come on, you spent your childhood here. You must know him. He can sometimes be a bit of a pest, especially when he takes my tools. But he is often good company.'

'You're right. He was here. It took me a while to recognise him. Last time I saw him I was a child. He was my playmate and when I got older, I sometimes wondered if he was an imaginary friend,' she said before adding, 'I was so lonely you see.'

The sympathetic look Harry gave her almost brought Deedee undone. It must have been returning home, the worry associated with her aunt, and now the talk of intruders, but she felt herself becoming quite emotional. Unaccustomed feelings washed over her and, giving herself a mental shake, Deedee desperately tried to find a way of changing the subject. With Bertie's recent words in mind, she continued.

'There was one thing Bertie said that concerned me Harry,

and I wonder if he has mentioned it to you. Mind you, it feels a bit odd to be recounting a conversation held with a ghost, but I suppose there is no reason why ghosts can't interact with the living. I suppose I didn't dream it all up.'

'No way. He's as real as you and me. Wait a minute, that came out wrong! He exists somehow, and I don't know why, but he is definitely here in this garden—his 'home'. If he is in the mood, Bertie will choose to appear—but not to everyone. Spit it out. What did he say? Nothing nasty I hope.'

'No, nothing nasty. I don't think he is that sort of ghost. He just mentioned strangers, or maybe it was *a* stranger, coming into the yard, entering via the gate from the river side, after dark— wandering around and writing things in a notebook.'

Harry's forehead wrinkled as if in reflection of the painful thought processes his mind was currently undertaking.

'That's news to me. I haven't seen anyone here and I've been here a bit while your aunt has been in hospital. After dark you say? And snooping around? Clearly not a social call then. Let me see. I can get a padlock for the front gate—one of those code ones—so those in the know can let themselves in. Mind you, it won't stop someone leaping the gate. Some motion sensor lights strategically placed might also do the trick. Leave it with me. I'll hit the hardware shop this arvo and get the stuff.'

Seeing Deedee's protesting gesture, he added: 'It's no trouble. I'll keep the receipt and you can fix me up later. It's just I don't like the idea of some stranger creeping around here and frightening the old lady. And yes, I do believe Bertie if he has told you this. He is a bit of a guardian of this place. Even my granddad knew him, said he was his playmate when he was little.'

As they wandered up the path back to the cottage, Harry shared all that he knew about Bertie. Seen by all the family from time to time, it was thought that Bertie was some relative from long ago— possibly his granddad's uncle. At least that is what Harry's granddad had told him.

'The family didn't have much luck growing children to adulthood in those days. Not unusual for the time, but they seemed to cop it worse than others. So, my Great Grandpa was one of four children—two girls and two boys. I got the impression that Bertie died young under mysterious circumstances. Those people in the family that might have known what had happened were long gone by the time any of us arrived and could ask. Grandpa just said no one talked of the past—about the dead Bertie or the girls. It's funny, you know. The girls are buried in the graveyard at the church. I'll show you sometime if you are interested. But there is no grave there for Bertie. Sometimes I wonder if that is why he hangs around in the garden, especially near that old elm tree. I wonder if perhaps he is buried somewhere nearby. And if so, does that mean he came to a messy end and no one was meant to know what had happened? It was pretty straightforward what happened to the girls—everyone else was dropping like flies with that Spanish flu. Poor Eloise and Cicely, they were just two of many that died at that time, leaving only my Great Grandpa who somehow not only survived but flourished. I guess because there was now more food to go around. Tough times eh?'

'Eloise and Cicely? I've heard those names before,' Deedee mused. The names seemed so familiar and without trying, she could conjure images of their faces to mind. Old fashioned faces that were consistent with their names—one with a cranky expression and the other rather dreamy looking.

'It's almost like I know them. Like I've met them somewhere. Maybe Minnie has told me stories about these relatives of yours. It must be strange having so much of your family's history wrapped up in this place, yet seeing strangers live here.'

'Not at all! You forget I've known Minnie and Alice for years—since I was little. It's almost like this is an extension of my home and they've become sort of family—just as bossy and interfering as are the rest of my relatives. That might be why I like coming here to help the old girl out—that and for a dose of her sparkling wit! But maybe not her cooking skills. I smell burning.'

Chapter Eleven

By the time they reached the side door, the smell of burnt toast was evident. Minnie was fussing in the kitchen, trying to scrape charred fragments off a pile of blackened toast.

'There you are,' she said once she caught sight of Harry and Deedee. 'Maybe you can rescue this toast. I forgot it you see. I thought I would make us some toast to go with the soup for lunch. But I got distracted and you can see what happened.'

With trembling hands, she gestured to the unappetising charred remains of what should have been part of their lunch.

'No problem,' said Harry in a calming voice. 'I'll duck up the road and get some rolls from the bakery. Won't be a tick and you two can sort out the soup while I'm gone. Problem solved!'

The soup was delicious. A hearty vegetable and bean concoction on which they sprinkled grated parmesan cheese and parsley. They all agreed that the freshly baked bread rolls were the perfect partner to their meal and so much better than any toast could have been— burnt or otherwise.

With soup bowls wiped clean with the last of the bread rolls, they relaxed over a shared pot of tea. Deedee saw it as the perfect opportunity to try and ferret some information out of Minnie about the reported intruder—in a subtle way of course. So as not to alarm her aunt, she started by asking about the local gossip. But she had grossly underestimated Minnie's suspiciousness.

'It's not like you to be interested in what's going on in this town. What are you after Deedee dear?'

'Nothing Aunt. I was just making a bit of conversation.'

'Again, not like you at all. I'm usually the one trying to drag information out of *you*. You're way too quiet to indulge in idle chitchat. Something is going on. Tell me.' Her aunt's eyes glared along with her command, leaving Deedee feeling like the small child she once was, surrender having become inevitable. But before she could speak, Harry came to the rescue.

'Minnie, my fault. I thought there was an intruder in the garden the other evening when I was packing up to go, but they weren't here long enough for me to see who it was. I told Deedee and we were just wondering if this had happened before.'

It was clear this information came as no surprise to Minnie as she didn't seem concerned, more like it had settled something she had already suspected. Her response confirmed this.

'An intruder you say? Well, I suppose I'm not surprised. All sorts of things are going on at the moment. I really didn't want to worry you Deedee, but now that you ask, I suppose you are entitled to know. And you too Harry. This was once your family's home after all.'

Taking a deep breath, Minnie continued with her story. It turned out that not that long before she had been approached by the local real estate agent who told her he had some businessmen clients who were interested in buying her cottage.

'Taking it off my hands, as if he was doing me a favour,' she said. Of course, she told him no. Coming so soon after Alice's death, the last thing Minnie wanted to do was contemplate change. 'As if I could leave here. This is where all my memories are—living with Alice, bringing you up Deedee. All the love and laughter trapped in these walls—and the sorrow too,' she added in a more serious tone. 'How could I leave? So, I told him in no uncertain terms to go away and not to bother me again.'

But the contact had unfortunately continued. First, he had

written to her confirming the offer, then some stranger came at her in the garden late one afternoon wanting to discuss a possible purchase.

'He gave me a fright that one did. It was just on dusk and I was out doing a bit of weeding—not that you would notice where I had been. It's all so neglected. Next thing I know the cat is hissing. A bit unusual I thought. I turn around and there he is, just standing there staring at me. He could have been there for ages for all I know. He was so quiet. It gave me the creeps. No wonder the cat reacted. Anyway, I asked him what he wanted. He was polite. Introduced himself—some double-barrelled name—and explained he wanted to buy my home. Made me an offer—more money than I have ever seen in my life—and said I could live out my days here as part of the deal. He calmly told me he had the money to meet my every demand. As if mere money would be sufficient to seal the deal!'

Minnie shook her head and continued.

'But I wasn't tempted. It wasn't the money—I think he would have given me more if I was prepared to bargain. It was more than that. You see there was something about him. You know, a whiff of something not quite right about him. Not only had he given me a fright, but I could see my cat objected to him—back arched, fur on end, and hissing. He doesn't often do that. And that boy—you know the one Harry? Well, he was doing his best to scare him off by pelting him with berries. Had no effect mind you, but I could see the boy didn't trust him either. So, I drew myself up to my intimidating height of five foot, and with my poshest accent I told him to leave. And he did. But not before promising to return. I haven't seen him back here again. Mind you, I haven't been here that much. And to be honest, I really don't want to see him again. There was something about him ...' Minnie's voice trailed off as she carefully set down her cup, clutched with now trembling hands.

It was the sight of those trembling hands that affected Deedee. Her aunt was not one to be easily scared. More often than not, she was the one doing the frightening. Deedee could clearly recall this from her childhood. How dare this man intimidate a little old lady! An old lady who might think she can make herself imposing at five foot fully stretched, but as any impartial observer would clearly see, in reality she was a tiny, frail shadow of her former self.

'How dare he frighten you Minnie! That does it! We're not having him back again. Harry, I think you are right—a lock on the front gate, and maybe the side gate, and some of those motion sensor lights you were talking about. That would be excellent. How dare this person harass you! Never mind Aunt, he now has the two of *us* to deal with.'

It was a measure of Minnie's intimidation by this stranger that she did not object to the added security arrangements. But she did want to know how the locks would be opened—was there a key? Seemingly satisfied with the explanation that they would be combination locks, she nodded her consent. They all agreed that this would be sufficient for the time being, but Harry also offered to keep an eye on the place and lend them his dog who was a known barker.

'No thank you, Harry. I think we will be fine for now. Deedee makes sure the doors are locked each night and Scruff, lovely visitor that he is, might upset Merlin if he did move in for a longer stay. I can also rely on the boy in the garden to scare any intruders away, and if they get inside, I'm sure Eloise and Cicely will do their bit. They used to terrify you when you were little Deedee, remember?'

Those names again. It was clear she was expected to be familiar with whomever they were. But who were they? The puzzlement was clearly obvious on Deedee's face as her aunt, giving a chuckle, explained.

'This is an old house my dear. It has lived many lives. Some of those lives continue—in parallel with us. I'm not sure why but that's how it is. If you treat them nicely, they will respect you. Although, it is a bit too much to ask Eloise and Cicely to be kind—especially Eloise—but so long as you are polite, they won't be too difficult. The boy though, he is just wild, a bit like the garden I suppose.'

Memories of terrifying ethereal ladies inhabiting the front sitting room with their fusty scent of talcum powder, came flooding back. Neither of them was particularly welcoming nor tolerant of a little girl—one just slightly less so. No wonder she felt reluctant to enter that room when she returned the other day. Some subconscious recollection of the terror they had invoked in the young Deedee's mind still lingered. But her aunt was correct, those old ladies did not welcome visitors, and could no doubt be relied upon to send a chill up the spine of any intruder who might come to call.

'Now I remember. Those scary spirit ladies who hated little children—or any stranger at that.'

Turning to Harry, Minnie continued.

'You know Harry, they are most likely some sort of relatives of yours. Are their names familiar?'

'Definitely,' Harry grinned. 'All my *living* aunts are scary, so I guess there's no reason why the *dead* aunts would not be the same. Must be a family thing, I guess. I'm fairly certain they're the two maiden aunts I was telling you about earlier Deedee. You know the ones who died from the Spanish flu. Probably died in that front room, which might explain why they still linger. Sisters of Bertie. Although, he died when he was much younger. If they're as terrifying as you and Minnie say, I really don't think I want to meet them—relatives or not.' Harry looked around the room, eyes crinkling in amusement. 'My, this house is rather crowded. Are you sure there is no one else in residence?'

With a snort of laughter and a wave of her hand, Minnie shushed him.

'Horrible boy. Where's your respect? Now, speaking of respect, it's time you paid attention to this old lady and got back to your work. This isn't a party, you know. You have a job to do.'

Harry pushed his chair away from the table and went to stand up.

'Actually, I've done enough around here for today. You can now access the studio, and I will be back in the next day or so to do a bit more trimming. If I can get to the hardware shop this afternoon, I'll be back before dark to sort out some locks for the gates. But I also have lawns to cut this afternoon, so I give no promises. Now, if you ladies would please excuse us, Scruff and I will get out of your hair.'

After Harry had left, and once the lunch dishes had been stacked in the dishwasher, Minnie made a show of insisting on inspecting the work completed by Harry that day. However, she didn't fool her niece. It was so obvious she really wanted to inspect the studio. Not a place Deedee wished to return to, given its memories of Alice, but she decided that if her aunt could manage it, so could she.

Arm in arm they progressed slowly along the garden path, Minnie pausing every now and then to inspect a plant, snip off a spent flower, or simply just to bend over and smell a spring blossom. Their progress was slow. They had walked like this so many times in the past, yet Deedee could not recall her aunt being so slow or taking such small, deliberate steps. Nor could she recall a time before when she could feel the leaden weight of her aunt as she leaned on her arm, as if needing her support for balance. Or even, when they finally reached the studio, taking such care to manoeuvre herself onto the front step. These were all signs of impending fragility that Deedee had not anticipated, nor welcomed. Her aunt, standing in the doorway, paused and looked around the room. The studio now cleared of most of the cobwebs, was cluttered with the detritus of an artist's life—two half-painted canvases resting on easels, and blank canvases stacked against the wall as if waiting to be brought to life. Minnie carefully stepped into the room and headed straight for the worn armchair where, with some deliberation, she sat and looked thoughtfully around the room.

'It's almost as if Alice is still here with us. Like she's just popped out into the garden for a moment and will be back shortly to continue working on that painting,' Minnie said gesturing to one of the half-painted canvases. It appeared to be a landscape depicting a meandering river and lush paddocks.

'You know, after Alice died, I couldn't bring myself to come up here. Yet now that I'm here, I wonder why I stayed away. It really is a lovely place, and so peaceful—a bit like Alice herself. I didn't want to tidy her stuff away and now I can see why. I'm sure Deedee, dear Alice would want you to use this studio and enjoy it as much as she did. What do you think about that?' A pair of beady eyes considered Deedee, a bit like a spider contemplating its prey.

Deedee felt trapped. What else could she do but agree? This was not the time to upset her aunt. Maybe in time she might come to enjoy working here. After all, it was just the sort of place any artist would dream of—purpose built, light and airy, and with room for paints and storage aplenty. She wandered around the room, picking up paint brushes and putting them down again, standing in front of the unfinished painting and considering, not just the painting, but how to respond to her Aunt Minnie.

'Of course. This is a perfect studio. I have so many happy memories of being up here with Alice—from when I was little really. Being beside her working on my paintings but also watching Alice at work. She taught me so much. It's like I can still hear her voice in here, her advice guiding my hand.' A smile lit up Deedee's face and was soon reflected in her aunt's eyes. 'You know, maybe you're right. I once thought we should leave Alice's studio alone. But when I think of all the times I shared this space with her in the past, well it makes me think I can still do so. Mind you, I don't want to move Alice's stuff out, more like make a corner for me. Maybe she will continue to inspire me like she used to.'

The old lady and her great-niece smiled at each other in shared understanding. Life would continue in the studio. It was just that Minnie and Deedee had different concepts as to how long this artistic life would exist in this location. Deedee was still intending her stay to be a short one, but Minnie had other ideas.

Chapter Twelve

That night Minnie, pleading exhaustion, was in bed by 9:00 pm. It was a bit of a lie as she was not at all exhausted. What Minnie really wanted was some time by herself to lie in bed and think—process all that had been happening in recent weeks and make her plans. She wasn't entirely on her own. Merlin had quietly followed her into the bedroom and was now curled up beside her on the bed. Minnie thoughtfully stroked the big black cat from head to toe. He responded by turning up the volume on his purrs.

'That's quite enough from you, old boy. You'll wake the dead with all that noise. Shoosh and let me think.'

Shifting carefully in an attempt to ease the persistent ache in her right hip, Minnie looked thoughtfully across the room. This had always been the guest room and had been furnished by Alice and herself with care to create a welcoming place for their visitors. But there weren't many visitors these days. At her age, the friends that used to visit were either dead or infirm and confined to residential care or whatever politically correct name they gave it. Still, there were memories that each item in the room invoked. The four-poster cedar bed was a treasure Alice had located in a local antique shop. The old washstand in the corner—no idea where that had come from, maybe it had always been there. It certainly looked like it was in no state to be moved—all rickety and battered—a bit like her come to think about it. And the worn but comfortable chair that even Minnie could now visualise as providing a resting place for her father at the end of each day when it had once sat in his home.

With a mental shake, Minnie refocussed. There was no time to dwell on the past. She had a great-niece to sort out. It was clear to Minnie she didn't have long left in this world and in a way, that was something she welcomed. Life without Alice had become so dreary. But she felt she could not leave Deedee until such time as she was settled. Something was wrong with that girl. She was not happy. Yet Minnie knew that if she asked Deedee directly what the matter was, she would deny it outright. She would point to her successful career, her independence, her happy home and loving friends, and try to soothe her aunt. But Minnie was not so easily fooled. The sad look in her niece's eyes, and sheer lack of enthusiasm about the art that once was her reason for living, told another story. And what had happened to the man that used to feature in every second sentence? There had been no mention of him, nor did she speak of any replacement. That was a worry for as far as Minnie was concerned, a partner was what her great-niece truly needed.

With that in mind, she mulled over the day's events. Young Harry in particular. It hadn't escaped her at lunchtime how at ease Harry and Deedee were with each other. How they chatted like long lost friends which, in a way, they could have been she supposed. Although, they more like long lost acquaintances when she thought about it. Still, there appeared to be a spark between the two of them. Minnie liked the way Harry seemed to be concerned about their welfare, and it hadn't escaped her how Deedee looked to him for advice. Maybe she should take a matchmaker's role and find reasons to encourage Harry to visit. After all, there was still so much to do in the garden. Surely Deedee would not be suspicious if she arranged for Harry to do some more work. Even if her niece decided she didn't enjoy the young man's company, it was still fun for this old lady to have a young man looking after her—especially such a handsome young man! Despite the fact that he insisted on bringing that scruffy dog with him, his company was always a welcome diversion.

With a smile on her face and a shove to the cat who was now lying diagonally, Minnie wriggled herself into a more or less comfortable position and dozed off. Unbeknown to her niece, a solution to Deedee's problems had now been identified and all would be well.

*

A doctor's appointment had been scheduled for the following morning and despite Minnie's resisting and saying that she was 'perfectly fine', Deedee managed to persuade her to get into the car and they headed for the doctor's surgery.

'I don't need to see the doctor. You know that. I feel perfectly well. I'm eating and resting, and I have you to look after me if I need looking after—which I don't!' grumbled Minnie.

Deedee, focussing on the traffic, agreed, which made it hard for Minnie to continue with the argument.

As usual, the doctor's surgery was awash with people. Children squirming and whining, uttering complaints that the adults were also thinking and wished they could say out loud. Above it all, from its place high on the otherwise blank wall, a large TV screen droned with mindless reporting by some generic blonde number. Deedee settled her aunt into a chair, gave her some well-thumbed magazines, and sat beside her surrendering to the thought of a long wait. Surprisingly, it wasn't as long as she had expected. A young doctor called her aunt's name and directed her down the corridor. Her aunt, with an unexpectedly strong grip, grasped Deedee's arm and hissed, 'You wanted me to see him so you're coming in with me. You're not getting out of it that easily. If I have to suffer, so do you.' Then, turning towards the beckoning doctor, Minnie put on what she considered to be a friendly expression—to Deedee it looked rather ominous—and she greeted the young man.

'On my way doctor. I'm a bit slow these days. How are you? I'm bringing my great-niece in with me. I'm sure you won't mind.'

As if he had a choice. Deedee smiled to herself. Her aunt might be a bit wobbly on her feet, but her strong will was still unassailable.

The doctor's examination was straightforward. He started by asking how her aunt was feeling. Minnie's answer was predictable.

'Perfectly fine young man. I didn't want to waste your time but my niece here—well, great-niece actually—insisted. Young ones can be so pushy.'

The doctor looked at Deedee, appearing to be quite alarmed. Maybe thoughts of elder abuse were circulating in his brain. Deedee did her best to smile back at him reassuringly and tried to look as lovingly as possible towards Minnie, as her aunt continued.

'I know I had a bit of a turn recently and while I really appreciate the excellent care I received in the hospital; you can see for yourself that I am fine. I am eating and sleeping just as I should, so I expect you won't want to see me again.'

It was clear Minnie had no time for doctors or their surgeries. Not even the doctor's cautions after checking her blood pressure had any impact on Minnie.

'Ms Green. Your blood pressure continues to be high. It is at the same level as when I last tested you. I'm really concerned that something else is going on with you so I would like to arrange some further tests.'

Sensing her aunt's immediate objection to this proposal, Deedee jumped in and spoke.

'Certainly, doctor. Please give me the paperwork and I'll arrange it.'

Out of the corner of her eye, she could see her aunt glowering in Deedee's direction. This, and her now tightly crossed arms, did not bode well. Still, at least she was keeping silent—for now.

She wasn't so silent once they were back in the car and heading for home.

'I won't do it you know. No further tests. I'm as fine as I can be for my age.'

'But Aunt, your blood pressure.'

'So what? Something has to take me off and if it is something quick like a heart attack then so be it.' As Deedee went to say something further, Minnie continued. 'Deedee dear, don't fuss. This is my decision and not yours. Love you though I do, I have a horror of a long, slow decline. A quick end is all I wish for. Let's put all that paperwork the young doctor gave me into the fire and talk no more about it. I have a deal to propose. If you stop nagging about doctors and the like and just focus on cooking good food, I promise you I will eat, rest and be happy. Deal?'

What else could she do but agree. If her aunt's mind was made up, that was that. Deedee knew from experience that Minnie was stubborn, and it was only ever Alice that she listened to.

Harry's car was parked by the side gate when they drove up closer to home.

'Excellent,' said Minnie. 'Maybe Harry will be able to finish the gardening today. I really need him to do some other odd jobs while he is here.' She smiled with satisfaction. If she could get Harry to commit to spending more time here, everything might just fall into place. Still, she would need to take care not to be too obvious. No point making Deedee suspicious.

Little did Minnie know, Harry already had plans of his own. Seeing Deedee the other day had reminded him of the times so long ago when he had felt protective of that young girl. How lost and alone she had seemed, and how vulnerable she was to the bullying antics of Libby. He still remembered how fired up he had been when he came across the cowering child. And like a knight to the rescue, he had stormed in and swept her to safety. Come to think of it, even though Libby was not some ferocious, fire breathing dragon, but it was clear she had terrified Deedee, and that had been enough to awaken his protective instincts. In the intervening years, he had seldom seen Deedee and if he had, it had only been in passing. The directions they had each taken in their lives and careers had diverged, and to be honest, he had rarely, if ever, thought of her. Occasionally, when making polite conversation with Minnie and Alice on one of his gardening visits, he would ask after Deedee, but their responses were usually quickly forgotten—if they ever even registered. But since stumbling into Deedee the other day in the garden, thoughts of her had lingered in his mind. Not only because the adult Deedee was amazingly appealing to him with her wild, black curls and dark mysterious eyes—so different to his own fair colouring—but also because those earlier protective instincts had reawakened. For some reason, he sensed that this young woman still needed care and protection, just like she did all those years ago.

These were the musings that he was tossing over in his mind, just as he was tossing over the clods of soil in the garden when Deedee appeared with a mug of coffee and a plate of biscuits. Handing him the mug and setting the plate on a nearby flat rock, she stood back and observed Harry. Still dressed in his work-stained shirt with logo, and grubby jeans, he looked exactly as he should— strong yet grubby—but a welcoming grubby as he looked up and greeted her approach with a happy grin. His face was content as he took one long and sustained slurp of the coffee.

'Thanks. I needed that. You're a lifesaver. Digging gardens is such thankless work, but necessary. I'm sure Madame Minerva will want to plant something here now that it is dug over. I've done the gates though. Want to see?'

'Sure. We might as well look while you have a break and stretch out your back and legs.'

'Good idea. You bring the biscuits.'

Both gates now sported impressive looking chains secured by a combination padlock.

'I've also put in some solar powered motion lights just inside the gates. They should come on with any movement and alert you. Not one hundred per cent sure you are going to thank me for that. With all the possums in the neighbourhood, you might find they are constantly triggering the lights. But I guess time will tell.' With a laugh, he continued, 'And who knows if they will register our little friend. Young Bertie I mean. Now that might be something! Maybe you could run ghost tours.'

'Hah! No way! Do you think any of the inhabitants of this cottage and garden, living or dead, would be that co-operative, appear on command and interact with visitors? I think not! Here, give me that mug. I have work to do. Minnie is demanding I make her a decent lunch—whatever that is. And then I am going to paint this afternoon. She's convinced me to use the old studio, so I need to get started.'

'She can be a hard taskmaster. Don't let her boss you around too much.'

'In a way, it's a bit of a relief to see my aunt being her usual bossy self.' Deedee smiled and continued, 'She gave me a bit of a fright with that turn and all, and I suspect she is still not fully recovered—not that she'll fully admit that. I try not to let on how I feel. But at times like this, I wish Alice was still with us. She'd know what to do,' she said looking out thoughtfully across the garden and seeing, yet not really seeing, the beauty of the blossom and blooms that surrounded her.

'Don't you worry. Just you being here with Minnie is the best medicine for her. She really missed you, especially after Alice died. But I bet she never told you that. Anyway, she's asked me to do some work on the old house. There are a few repairs needed, or so she says. I'll be around if you need me. I'll give you my phone number and ...' He broke off and looked at Deedee as if he wasn't sure how to continue.

'And?'

'I was just wondering if you fancied joining me at the pub tonight. Nothing fancy—a drink and some of the gourmet burger stuff they serve for dinner. We can exchange phone numbers and catch up—away from here, away from talk about chores, and away from any interruptions by curious aunts. I see one such aunt heading this way.' He twinkled at Deedee as he gestured towards Minnie making slow but stately progress along the path, preceded by a dignified black cat.

'You're on,' Deedee laughed. 'Why not?'

Minnie, observing the interaction between these two people who, each in their own way were special to her, also smiled. Things were progressing exactly as she had planned.

That evening, Deedee was surprised when her aunt readily accepted her suggestion that she eat her supper on a tray in front of the TV and not wait up for her.

'I won't be late Aunt, but I'd be more relaxed knowing you weren't waiting up for me. I can take a key, and you and that cat won't have to listen out for me.'

Minnie tried hard not to look too happy at the prospect of her niece going out. Avoiding eye contact so Deedee couldn't see the joy sparking from her eyes, she focussed on some infinitesimal flaw in her knitting.

'It's fine dear. You young ones need to go out and socialise. Don't you worry about Merlin and me. We will be fine here, just like we always are. Anyway, I hear the pub is pretty fancy these days, so I will be interested in hearing your feedback. Maybe we should both try it out one day.'

'You're on. If I like it there tonight, I will take you there for a meal—maybe a lunch?'

Chapter Thirteen

Deedee had arranged to meet Harry at the pub at 7:00 that evening. As it was only three blocks up the road, she saw no point in driving there or being picked up. Allowing ten minutes to walk there, she bid her aunt goodnight with a soft kiss on a scented wrinkled cheek, and let herself out, making sure the door was locked securely behind her and the porch light was left on. Being the city girl that she was, Deedee had initially rejected her aunt's suggestion of taking a torchlight with her. But at her aunt's insistence, she had capitulated. It only took a few steps along the path for Deedee to appreciate her aunt's wisdom. After leaving the darkness of the garden the path, she soon realised that along the street was also dark, the streetlights scattered too far apart to be of any assistance. Shining the torchlight straight ahead and trying to avoid tripping over tree roots that were reinterpreting the path, she decided that if Harry were to offer her a lift home, she would certainly accept.

The pub was located a short way up the main street. A two-storey building with a wide street frontage, it dominated the streetscape. A verandah edged with decorative metal lacework overhung the footpath below. Above the verandah, the roof pediment sported decorative urns looking like they were intended to be the receptacles for the ashes of long departed publicans. And maybe they were. In the daytime, the building still retained its imposing effect on the neighbouring single-storey shops, albeit in a slightly rundown and raffish way. But at night-time, it wasn't possible to see the paint flaking off the external walls, or the rotting timberwork. The twinkling lights adorned the upstairs verandah rails, and the people spilling out of the downstairs rooms onto the front footpath all contrived to give it the appearance of a welcoming party place. Deedee, approaching from down the street, slowed down. Turning off the torch once she got closer, she hesitated. She now wondered why she had agreed to this outing. Apart from Harry, there was no one else here that she would know. If she couldn't find him in this crowd, she would feel like a right fool. She had never been much of a party person, preferring to linger in the shadows and observe others rather than being the centre of the crowd. With a sinking feeling, she started to wonder if maybe she had made the wrong decision. Glancing down at her outfit, she consoled herself that she at least would blend in. Faded jeans, a cropped top and denim jacket completed her look. A pearl pendant that had been a 21st birthday gift from Minnie and Alice, hung around her neck. She tried to still the feelings of panic as she peered at the mass of people crowding the footpath. *Where was he? Was she brave enough to go inside?*

Then, suddenly out of the muddle of noise, came a distinct sound—the sound of her name being called by a familiar voice.

'Deedee, over here.'

The anxious feeling lessened as she looked towards the open door and discerned a hand waving furiously over the crowd.

'Stay right there. I'll come over.'

Just like the seas parting for Moses, the crowd separated, and Harry strode through, smiling and laughing at people as he went. Her feelings of relief might almost have been as great as those felt by Moses. A feeling of being saved and no longer being out of her depth in a social situation that was beyond her. Harry drew nearer, his face beaming a warm welcome. Taking her by the hand, he drew her closer, gave her a hug and a peck on the cheek, and led her back into the crowd.

'I've been looking out for you. Figured you'd never find me in this crowd. Glad you made it though. Now if you don't mind, I thought we would go upstairs. There's a bit of a bistro up there. It's quieter and we can get something to eat. Nothing fancy though. It's a pub after all.'

They went through the solid timber front door and up a rather grand staircase that curved around so that when they reached the top they faced towards the street. Harry led her into a large room that opened onto the verandah. Deedee, looking around, couldn't help but gasp as she took in the ornate plaster cornice and decorative central ceiling picked out in various colours of rose and leaf green.

'Wow, this is amazing,' she said turning around and taking in the grandeur of the room.

'Yep. It's pretty good,' came the response from one obviously accustomed to its beauty. 'Get an eyeful of the floor. Amazing timber, isn't it? They're the original floorboards—a bit battered but look at that grain, and the colour.'

Deedee smiled as she considered the wide hardwood boards underfoot that were burnished and battered from over a hundred years of wear. She thought Harry couldn't have been any prouder of the building than if he had constructed it himself.

'It is lovely but I'm actually starving. Can we order and then admire the architecture later?'

It was exactly as Harry had explained. Pub food. But that was just what she wanted. They ordered gourmet hamburgers and hand cut chips, to be enjoyed with beer from a local boutique brewery. As they waited for their meals to arrive, Deedee quizzed Harry about his life. There was so little she knew about him. Apart from the vague memory of him being her childhood saviour and the knowledge that her aunt seemed to rely on him, his life was an unknown quantity. She thought he might be a kind person judging by the way Merlin and Scruff interacted with him. And easy going—maybe? He certainly wasn't fussed by Minnie's demands and she was yet to see him looking other than calm and, well, smiley. There was a lot to learn about this person who had been connected to her life for so long yet, when she thought about it, was a complete stranger.

Their meals arrived and ss they tucked into them, Harry spoke at length about his family—a mother and father with whom he still lived on the family farm, an older brother who worked on the farm alongside his father, and a sister who lived not that far away—a sister some eight years younger than him who was still completing her studies at a university in Canberra.

'That's if she ever does finish. I think she likes the student life and might end up being perpetually enrolled in something or other. Mum keeps hoping she'll find a farmer somewhere near here and move home, but I suspect that is the last thing Martha has in mind. She comes home fairly regularly, but she seems quite happy living in Canberra. I don't think she misses rural life at all.'

Under Deedee's questioning, Harry spoke at length about the farm—about its beauty and isolation.

'It's rather big you see, quite a few thousand acres. So, the neighbours are a way away, down the road or across the river.'

'The river?'

'Yeah. One of the boundaries is the Murrumbidgee River, which gives us water for irrigation of the crops and for our stock—and the dams of course. It's really beautiful, and if you're interested, I'll show you some time. Mind you, I should warn you that the parents will have lots of questions—about everything. I'm not sure if they've ever actually met you, but like people from all small communities, they will know everything about you. And by everything, I really do mean most things—especially your early days, your parents and all. Now that I think about it, I suspect my mum might have known your mother—from their student days maybe? That may or may not be a good thing for you. So, I suppose I won't mind if you decide you don't want to see the farm after all.'

That was something Deedee had not expected. It was not unreasonable to suspect that people here might have once known her mother. After all, her mother had spent some time living with Minnie when she was a young woman, and before she met Deedee's father, so there must have been times when both her parents had visited and brought Deedee along. As she stared back at Harry and considered her reaction to his words, she decided that meeting someone who once knew her mother mightn't be so bad after all. Her memories of her mother were so scattered and random. Meeting someone who might have different memories might help her complete the picture of her mother.

'I'd like to meet your parents. Really, I would,' she added in response to Harry's disbelieving look. 'I know so little about my past, or my mother's past, that anything extra I can learn would help.'

'It's strange, isn't it? The difference between our stories. Mine so boring and predictable. Apart from a few years away at uni, I've lived in the same home all my life. My parents and siblings have always been with me, no gaps in the story. If by any chance I forget something, I can rely on the siblings to set me straight! It's hard for me to imagine a life populated by so many gaps and that terrible loss of family history. If Mum can help, I'm sure she will.'

The caring expression on Harry's face almost brought Deedee undone. This discussion of aspects of her life that for so long she had kept shut away, was stirring up emotions she didn't know how to handle. At a loss for words, Deedee stared down at her hands clenched in her lap. How to respond to these well-meaning words? But before she could assemble her scattered thoughts into a coherent response, a voice intruded.

'My, fancy seeing you here Harry. And not on your own— imagine that. With a date and all. And so serious too. I hope I'm not interrupting a heart to heart. But there you are. Maybe I am. Too bad. Do introduce us.'

The voice, so smooth and with each syllable distinctly articulated, flowed across the table like so many musical chimes.

Deedee looked up and contemplated the woman standing next to Harry, flanked by another. They were like chalk and cheese. The woman, so blonde and elegant in a well-groomed, sophisticated way, was dressed like Deedee in jeans and a casual top, but somehow her attire made Deedee seem scruffy. Was it something to do with the dainty flowers embroidered up each trouser leg, or the way her blonde hair shone and moved like silk as she tossed her head? The man, tall dark and brooding—a bit like a Heathcliff come to life in modern times, wore a black leather bomber jacket echoing the swarthiness of his colouring and the glint of a two-day growth. No happenstance there. This wasn't a man who had forgotten to shave, but rather someone who prized the artifice of the contrived facial hair.

It was clear Harry did not welcome the interruption. But with his usual courtesy, he stood up and shook hands with the man and gave the woman a quick peck on the cheek.

'Hi there. I wasn't expecting to see you both here. I'm catching up with my friend Deedee. Libby, you'd remember Deedee, wouldn't you? I seem to recall you were at junior school together. Not sure Deedee, that you would have met Libby's brother Julian though.

Deedee stared thoughtfully at the two people. So, this must be the dreaded Libby who had made her life hell for a short while all those years ago. Given that she herself had such little recollection of the incident, it was no surprise that Libby was staring at her blankly. The brother on the other hand, was gazing at her with intense interest. He looked like he already had some inkling as to who she was—but why?

'Deedee, you say? I can't say I remember having met you before, but then again, my time at school is pretty much a distant memory. I left the local school here fairly early on. My parents, you see. They felt I could do so much better elsewhere—and I did,' she smirked, but as if to soften the blow, she held out her hand. 'Pleased to meet you, I'm sure. Are you staying nearby?'

As Harry explained that Deedee was visiting her aunt Minnie, she could sense Julian's increased attention. As if he was switching on a light, his face lit up and, holding out a hand, he introduced himself.

'Hi there. Pleased to meet you. Yes, I'm Libby's brother, or half-brother I should say. Different surnames and all that. Ours is one of those complicated families. Anyway, Libs and I are both visiting for a few days, and we decided we needed a bit of time away from the olds, so we thought a quick drink at the pub was a good idea. Gives the parentals a bit of time out too,' he said, smiling conspiringly at his sister.

The conversation petered out soon after that. Harry had made it clear by his abrupt responses to Libby's questioning that he really didn't want to talk. Eventually, the hint was taken, and after exchanged goodbyes—effusive on Libby's part and monosyllabic on Harry's—the siblings moved on and out of the room. Harry exhaled in relief.

'Thank goodness that's over. They were the last people I expected to see here. And together too. Julian avoids this town like the plague and he and Libby generally aren't the best of friends. So, the idea of them ducking out for a quick drink together is just plain ludicrous. I wonder what's going on. And something *will* be going on as Libby is never straightforward—I should know!'

Deedee contemplated her dinner partner as she recalled how he had mentioned previously that he and Libby had once been an item. Considering Harry as he sat opposite her, she could see that he was looking unnaturally subdued, his normally cheerful expression absent.

'Are you okay? I get the impression it was a bit of a shock seeing them just now. Do you want to talk about it?'

And he did.

Deedee soon discovered that the relationship had ended not that long ago—last Christmas to be exact, and it had ended acrimoniously. They had been dating for some years, having met while Harry was still studying in Canberra, where Libby worked as a marketing manager at a local radio station. Once Harry had graduated and returned home, they had continued to see each other, but the challenges of a long-distance relationship had made an impact. Contact had dwindled to catching up on weekends, and not every weekend at that. By then Harry had started to have doubts about a future together. Conflict escalated, perhaps because Libby sensed his withdrawal from her, or it could just have been because their lives were going along different paths. It all came to a head over the Christmas period when Libby insisted Harry commit to her and move his business into Canberra so they could live together as a couple. Immediately, Harry knew it wasn't a future he desired. He explained to Libby that he could not live in a city and that the rural lifestyle surrounded by known people was all he wanted. The inevitable explosion followed, and harsh words were said. Deedee suspected that this was largely by Libby, as she couldn't imagine the Harry she was coming to know, ever being enraged. He certainly wasn't showing any signs of anger as he recounted what had taken place. He looked morose and was staring down at his hands. The pain was still apparent.

'That must have been a hard thing to do—to say no.'

'Hardest thing I've ever done,' came the mumbled reply. 'Sure, she could be a bossy thing and sometimes that got up my goat. But I didn't hate her. It's just I could see no shared future for us. My place is here and hers isn't, simple as that. Sometimes I wonder what she saw in me. Our lives are so different.' With a grimace, he looked up at Deedee and apologised.

'Sorry to have dumped all of that on you. It's all history now and I shouldn't have inflicted all that on you. Not fair on you.'

'Nonsense! That's what friends are for,' she replied, feeling indignant that this poor man felt he couldn't open up to another.

'Friends? I like that.'

The grin had returned, and with a push backwards he stood up and held his hand out to her.

'Come on. Let's get out of here. I'll walk you home. Moon's still out and I think I need to stretch my legs.'

They went down the stairs, out the front door and past some smokers clustered on the pavement. Harry exchanged greetings with a few who stared curiously at Deedee. None of them were anyone she knew but that was probably not surprising. After all, she had rarely spent any time in this town since she was a child. Apart from her aunts and Harry, the number of people she knew in this small community could be counted on the fingers on one hand.

They moved away and headed down the footpath, past shops shut and in darkness for the night. Harry reached for her hand and grasped it in his. She could feel the roughened work weathered callouses as his fingers wrapped around hers. His hand so firm but not enveloping, felt warm, dry and secure. A feeling she welcomed.

'Thanks,' he said. And in response to Deedee's muttered expostulation, he continued, 'No, I mean it. Thank you for being there tonight, for being so calm and polite and all. That's the first time I have seen Libby since Christmas and to be honest, I had been dreading seeing her and all. It's not that I missed her, it's just I thought seeing her again would remind me of all the pain I went through, and I suppose she did too. But having you there somehow made it easier. I feel like what Libby and I went through is now behind me and almost like it happened to some other person. You can't imagine how good that feels!'

'Actually, I think I can!'

'You too?'

Deedee nodded, but didn't say anything further. Somehow Harry understood that this was enough for now. He didn't press her to say more. She liked him for that and the way his hand gently squeezed hers providing an unspoken comfort. That was enough—for now. Words could come later.

They strolled along into the deepening night. The chill made Deedee glad she had thought to wear her leather jacket. Turning the corner into a side street where the streetlights were few and far between, she reached into her pocket for her torch and switched it on.

'Ah, you city girls. Can't cope with a bit of dark, eh?' Harry said, amusement clear in his voice.

'Not scared at all. We city girls fear nothing! Just don't want to scuff my new boots on a tree root. Appearance is everything, you know!'

Harry laughed and contented himself with pointing out some of the local sights, not that they were too obvious at this time of night.

'The Catholic Church is further up this road, on the top of the hill. It's a great view and an amazing historic building. My aunt lives nearby—over there actually,' he said while pointing to his left.

'And up that side street over there is where my best friend since primary school lives.'

No wonder he couldn't contemplate a life away from this place, Deedee thought. Harry was so connected to this place—his family, his friends, his work which, every day must further entwine him in his community of customers and connect him with the gardens he tended. Like a plant, he had settled his roots deep into this community and from the look of him, he appeared to be flourishing. With dawning sadness, Deedee contemplated her own situation—where was her special place? Where did she feel like she belonged? Her place and her people? All her life she had been on the move. Even her time spent here with her aunts could only be measured by several years, terminating when she moved onto boarding school and then onto arts school, and a career elsewhere. Where did she belong? Unlike Harry, she didn't know.

Pushing the stubborn gate open and entering the garden, a thought sprung into her mind—did it really matter? After all, tonight—just being here in this garden and staying in this quirky little cottage—felt right. It was home for now and maybe that should be enough.

The garden, dense with dark undergrowth, was still and almost vigilant with its silent regard of these two intruders. Just inside the gate, they both paused. Deedee to take several appreciative sniffs of the night air so deeply fragrant with the scent of spring, and Harry to glance around as if looking for danger.

'That's funny. The motion light hasn't come on,' he muttered. And then, with another step, the light flooded them and the garden.

'That's ok then,' he said. 'For a moment there I thought I had done something wrong with the installation. I'll see you to the door and on my way out, I'll lock the gate. Okay?'

'Okay. Or do you want to come in for a coffee?'

'Thanks, but no thanks. Gotta start early tomorrow. So, I won't linger. But hey, I meant it when I said I'd like to bring you out to the farm and introduce you to the folks. If you are okay about that. How about this weekend?'

Meeting his family? The thought suddenly seemed overwhelming—too much too soon—and yet, the chance to speak to his mum about her mother tipped the balance. She could do it and maybe even enjoy it. After all, any family that had produced a person like Harry couldn't be too scary, could they??

'Sure. That would be lovely,' responded Deedee, remembering her manners. 'Either day is fine for me. I can drive out there if you give me directions. Saturday or Sunday is fine with me.'

'No way. I'll pick you up. I have to come in Saturday morning to do some chores, so I'll collect you. Say about 11:00? We can go home, meet the folks over morning tea or lunch, then I might show you around. I have an idea I want to talk to you about.' Seeing Deedee's questioning look, he added, 'Nope, not now. I'll explain when we are out on the farm on the weekend. It can keep. You'll see. Goodnight. Thanks for tonight. It was fun, wasn't it, despite uninvited guests?' And with a peck on her cheek, a grin, and a farewell wave, he turned and strode down the path and into the darkness, the sound of his tuneless humming overwhelming the once silent night.

Closing the door gently behind her, Deedee made sure it was locked and moved quietly down the hall towards the kitchen, all the while mulling over the night's events. Overall, it had been fun despite the unexpected meeting with Libby and Julian. Time spent with Harry was entertaining. He was a bit of a mystery to her—a country boy yet a thinker. There was more to him than what first appeared. He wasn't boring at all. She smiled to herself as she remembered some of their unexpected conversations that night. Who would have thought he was a reader? A good thing she hadn't prejudged him when they first met. What did he want from her? Was he just being friendly to the great-niece of a person of whom he was clearly very fond? She could sense that the wounds from his recent break up with Libby were fresh, and he gave no indication of wanting anything from her. But his hand was so warm and his kiss on her cheek so gentle. Should she see any significance in those gestures? Or were they just a demonstration of friendship? He did welcome the idea of them being friends at one stage and anyway, what did she want? Her recent heartbreak was still so painful, and hadn't she sworn off all relationships as a result? And yet … why was Harry so keen to show her the farm and introduce her to his family? Was he just being friendly or was this more? And what about the mysterious secret he was going to share with her on the weekend? Was this an enticement to trap her, or was it something else?

These questions tumbled over each other in her head, yet without any resolution, she reached the end of the corridor to find her aunt asleep by the fire with Merlin at her feet, nestled into the folds of a hand-knitted lap rug. No early bed for her then. Minnie must have been waiting for her return. No doubt wanting to find out all the gossip. There was nothing else to do but wake her and get Minnie into bed. She couldn't leave her there all night.

Gently, she shook her aunt to semi-wakefulness.

'What?' came the mumbled response to the shaking.

'Aunt, wake up. You fell asleep by the fire. Come on. I'll help you to bed. It's late and we both need to be asleep.'

As Deedee helped her aunt stand upright and stagger to her bedroom and into bed, after having divested herself of minimal clothing, Deedee wondered what would have happened if she hadn't been there to help. Maybe she would have slept by the fire all night, or at least until the fire had burnt out and she had awoken with the increasing chill in the room. Would that have mattered anyway? She had a blanket and the cat. Yet somehow Deedee felt responsible, that she needed to be here to help. Some part of her resented this feeling of obligation, while the other part lectured her on her selfishness. Why did life have to be so complicated?

Chapter Fourteen

Despite not getting to sleep until late, Deedee woke up early, in time for the dawn chorus. She knew her aunt would be asleep for many more hours, but for some reason she felt wide awake and ready to face the day. No way could she roll over and resume her slumbers. There was nothing for it—she must get up and go for a run. Running wasn't something Deedee did every day; it was more a token activity to be undertaken three or four times a week in a forlorn attempt to maintain her fitness. She had no regular routine, and more often than not she would find an excuse not to have to brave the elements—too wet, too windy, too hot, or too cold. But this morning there was no such excuse. She felt rested, alive and in need of shaking out the fidgets—and maybe do some thinking. Deedee often found that once she settled into a rhythmic pace, that was when she did her best thinking. Somehow, she felt she needed to unravel and make sense of all the thoughts that were tangled in her mind. Those worries about her Minnie and what to do about her ongoing care. Then there was her speculation about Harry. Was there anything significant about his interest and if so, was it welcome?

She left the house through the side door and headed along the garden path to the front of the property. The gate opened onto the dusty footpath that wound alongside the river—typically a popular walking and running spot for the locals. But at this time of the morning, it was deserted. Just how Deedee liked it.

The morning was clear and cold, yet with a promise of warmth as the day progressed. There had been no frost the night before, just a heavy dew that clung to the bushes against which Deedee brushed as she jogged along the path, the dampness seeping into her leggings. The dirt and gravel track followed the bends of the river, sometimes straight, sometimes winding, and as deserted as the path may have been, it certainly wasn't silent. From time to time, the river sung as it chattered over the stony rapids, falling silent when it resumed its stately flow. At all times there was a cacophony of bird song—cheeping, tweeting, trilling, and screeching as the birds performed according to their individual song sheets.

Small fluttering birds—black with red eyes—choughs she thought—worked the leaf litter under the bushes at the edges of the path. They paid her no mind as she jogged along but they occasionally scuttled to the safety of the undergrowth when they considered she was a little too close. The screech of the yellow-crested white cockatoos flying overhead surely must have been loud enough to wake the entire town, but then again, maybe the locals were used to it.

As she ran, Deedee worked hard to clarify her thinking. She told herself it should be simple—her aunt, so frail and rapidly going downhill, clearly needed her. She loved Minnie without a doubt, and she owed her so much, even if sometimes she did annoy her with her bossy ways. So, what was holding her back? Was it the thought of going back to the aunt/child relationship of times long ago, or the responsibility of being a carer, or just the simple thought of moving back to a place that held so many memories of times long past—some happy and some sad? It wasn't like there was anything in Sydney that was anchoring her to that place. Her friends—well, there weren't that many, and if they were true friends, they would remain connected wherever she lived. Her home on Sydney's Northern Beaches, no matter how lovely it was, did not belong to her. It was a rental property that she could never afford to buy. She also no longer had a loved one in her life that could tie her to one spot. And there was no hope of a reunion. He had made it very clear that he saw no future in a shared life—he had turned his back and walked away on Deedee and her broken heart. So why was she hesitating? Was it because she was feeling like she was being backed into a corner? Or ... Deedee paused in her stride as she considered her new thought ... was it because she could see that the time left to spend with her aunt was diminishing with each day and she was terrified of losing her? Crouching over with her hands on her knees, trying to recover her breath, Deedee could feel the tears filling her eyes, and running down her sweat-sheened cheeks.

Was that it? Not only some selfishness at the thought of abandoning her Sydney life for another life not of her choosing, but also grief at the imminent loss of her last family member. A reminder that she would soon be the sole survivor of this family. There was no doubt that Alice's death earlier that year had been shocking, but there was a comfort in knowing that Alice's suffering was over, and she still had Minnie to nag, rouse and fuss over her. But this impending loss was so much more. In some ways the feelings she was experiencing were reminiscent of those she felt all those years ago when her parents perished—the feeling of being completely alone and bereft—yes, bereft!

Standing upright, pulse and breathing now having settled, Deedee worked through a series of stretches, feeling strangely reluctant to resume her jog.

There was a thudding of footsteps behind her as someone approached. Deedee moved to one side to allow the approaching person to pass by. As she continued with her stretches, she sensed the person drawing nearer, heard the footsteps slow, and recognised the voice calling out to her.

'Deedee, isn't it? We met last night. I wasn't expecting to see anyone else here so early this morning. But then again, it is a good morning to be out and about.'

Turning, Deedee considered the person approaching her. Tall and, judging by his attire—lycra jogging pants clinging tightly to nicely muscled legs, a zip-up windbreaker, and a fine woollen beanie covering what she recalled was wild dark hair, he was clearly no stranger to outdoor activities. His trendy, two-day beard was all she could recognise as familiar from the night before—that and those divine dark eyes now twinkling in her direction. Of course, he was the half-brother of the dreaded Libby. Now, what was his name again?

The problem was solved as he slowly put his hand out in introduction and said, 'Julian. We met last night. Julian Blakely-Hill is my full name, but I generally just get called 'Jules' or 'J' by my friends. Nothing too complicated. It is, Deedee isn't it? I didn't get that wrong, did I?'

Deedee nodded and took the proffered hand. There was a tingle, a buzz, as the two hands connected. His hand curved around hers and enclosed in a firm grip, releasing just as she registered the surge of electricity she was feeling. Then a sense of loss, an absence, as the feeling disappeared along with the withdrawal of his hand. Did she imagine it? Maybe it was just static from her clothes? But then, as he took her arm and led her to a nearby bench, there it was again—that sense of connection between the two of them.

Get a grip, she told herself, trying to remember her manners.

'Yes, I remember. We met last night at the pub. It was all a bit crowded so I'm not sure we talked much, but I seem to recall you were visiting your family just like I am.'

'Yeah, families! One reason why I am out and about so early this morning. I just felt like I needed some time to myself. Oops, that came out wrong.' He laughed, eyes twinkling with good humour. 'I meant it's time away from family, not time away from others. Really, I'm glad I ran into you again. It's odd, I feel like I should know you, but somehow our paths have never crossed. Tell me, where do you live?'

As Deedee explained how she was visiting her aunt but that she really lived in Sydney, she could sense Julian was far more interested in her current address than her Sydney one.

'Yes, I'm staying with my Great Aunt Minerva. Such a mouthful so I often just call her my Aunt Minnie. I used to live with Minnie and her partner when I was a child, that is why this is more a home to me than anywhere else.' Deedee pointed behind her in the direction of where she had come. 'Minnie's house is down this jogging track—by the river. Not far behind us really, but largely hidden by the overgrown garden.'

'I think I know which place you mean. Sort of mysterious the way it is hidden by all that greenery—like it belongs to another world. Actually, now that I think about it, I *do* know the place you mean. In fact, our family own the land that adjoins it. If you head in the other direction—past your aunt's house, or great aunt, or whatever you call her, you will see some river flats and more paddocks behind them. My parents still use them for their sheep, but they are under pressure to redevelop it for housing as it is on the edge of town. Progress I suppose.' He said the last sentence with a grimace and a shrug as if to also say: *What can you do? You can't fight progress.*

And then, with an intense look at Deedee, he changed the topic.

'Are you okay? You look like you might be a bit upset. Can I help?'

Deedee shook her head and wiped her still damp eyes with one hand.

'No. No. It's alright. I don't know what it is about jogging, but somehow it gets me to thinking and pondering stuff. Trouble is, it doesn't help me to find solutions. But really, I am okay,' she said with what she hoped was a reassuring smile.

Jules stood and stretched his arms above his head, then out to the side. He looked down at Deedee, and with one hand he reached out to her as if in invitation to help her up. Interested in feeling that hand again, she reached out—almost without conscious thought—as Jules clasped her hand and helped her upright. That tingle, that buzz, present again. *Could he feel it too?*

'Come on. Let's call it a day. You can only exercise for so long. I know a place that not only does good coffee, but also opens early. Let me buy you a coffee. I promise you it is excellent—good enough for a city girl like you.'

That electric smile again, this time slightly mischievous as if he were daring her not to accept. With his hand still clasping hers, Deedee could not find it in herself to refuse.

The coffee was, as promised, excellent. The quaint little shop was on the main street, not that far from where she had met Harry the previous night. It was in a single-storey, red brick building and given it was largely obscured by two adjoining, much larger buildings, it wasn't surprising that she hadn't noticed it before. There was a cosy fug inside, the place crowded with other early customers keen to start their day with a decent coffee. Jules and Deedee squeezed their way past customers queueing for their takeaway drinks and found a seat by the fire. Deedee couldn't help but laugh as Jules removed his beanie to reveal tangled dark hair flying in all directions. She pointed at his hair and laughed again.

'Your hair! You really give "hat hair" a bad name! Maybe better to leave the beanie on?'

'So superficial! Only care about outward appearances, do you?' he said while frantically trying to flatten his wayward hair—but to no avail. 'Never mind. You'll just have to accept the natural un-airbrushed me. That or I will put my beanie back on if it causes you too much distress. But …' There was that twinkle again. … Before you say anything further, you might want to consider your own appearance.'

Deedee stood up and looked into the mirror that hung over the fireplace. He was right! The bastard! Her hair, a mass of tangled curls, was no better.

'Okay, okay, I take back what I said. We are both so scruffy, it's a wonder if they serve us and don't just kick us out.'

'It's amazing what mere money can achieve,' he said complacently and for a moment, alarm bells rang in the back of Deedee's mind. Where had she heard something like that said before? Two mugs of steaming hot coffee arrived and the thought disappeared.

Between sips of the steaming drinks, they took turns in sharing details about themselves. Julian explained that he had been visiting his mother and stepfather for the last week, but he was keen to get back to his home in Sydney.

'As much as I love seeing the folks and catching up on their news, after a few days I find myself missing home and my routine. My job I can largely do remotely, but there comes a point where I do need to return—and that is rapidly approaching.'

Hearing this, Deedee felt the plummet of disappointment in her stomach. She had only just met this intriguing man and he was about to leave? She needed to know.

'Oh, that's a shame when we've only just met,' she said while mentally kicking herself. *Stupid, stupid girl—how pathetically needy you sound. Now, where is a hole I can crawl into and hide?*

But her words seemed to have been well received. With a sympathetic smile, Julian responded.

'Yeah, my timing is not terrific, is it? Still, I'm often back to see family. This time I am not heading off until possibly the day after tomorrow—Saturday or Sunday—so maybe we can go for another jog tomorrow morning. Then maybe breakfast? That is if you are not too busy.'

'I'd like that,' she said, realising it was in fact true. She really *did* want to see him again.

They made plans to meet early the following morning, outside the front gate of Minnie's house—by the river. Julian assured her that he knew the spot and would be there waiting. After exchanging phone numbers, they both left the café and headed off in separate directions—Julian up the road, and Deedee walking slowly back to Minnie's home. As she did so, she puzzled over her reaction to this man. That fizz of excitement when he drew closer. This physical reaction was something she had never experienced before. It was almost as if she was in close proximity with something, or someone, that could challenge or exhilarate her, the sort of feeling she got as she walked along the clifftops on a walk from Bondi to Tamarama. Yes, that was it! She remembered that thrilling sensation she experienced as she looked down the rugged cliffs, towards the waves smashing on the rock platform so far below. She felt like she was being urged to jump, and it was only with great strength of will that she was able to resist the siren call and draw herself back from danger. Now she was experiencing the same sensation. At some subliminal level, Deedee sensed that Julian spelled trouble. But yet, after that first touch, all her body desired was to be close to him again.

Turning the corner and heading up the dirt track, Deedee shook her head. *You're as bad as a young girl experiencing her first crush. How pathetic! But then again, why not?*

'Why not indeed?' she muttered to herself as she reached the gate and with a shove, pushed it open.

Even though it felt like she had been away for hours—perhaps because of the significant impact her recent interaction with Julian had had on her—it was still early morning by the time she returned home. With no sign of her aunt, Deedee presumed she must still be asleep in bed. She busied herself tidying up the kitchen, stacking the dishwasher, and preparing breakfast. A tray, set with a small pot of steaming Ceylon tea, a dainty cup and saucer with matching milk jug, and some buttered toast, was soon ready. Carefully, so as not to spill a drop, Deedee carried the tray to her aunt's bedroom. Balancing the tray on a nearby table, she knocked on the door and entered before her aunt responded.

'Here, I've brought you a cuppa and some toast. I'll make you a proper breakfast once you are up and about,' she said setting the tray on the adjacent bedside table and heading to the window to open the curtains.

Her aunt stirred. A thin arm reached to pull the quilt closer, and with a quavering voice she mumbled, 'Thank you dear. It seems awfully early. I'll take my time if you don't mind. In fact, I think this should do me for now. You go off and have your breakfast and please don't wait for me. I might just have this and then have a bit more of a sleep.'

'Of course, Minnie. Take your time. I've heaps to do. Once I've had a bite to eat, I'll be up in the studio. But I'll check in on you mid-morning in case you want something more.'

As she left Minnie's bedroom, Deedee tried hard not to worry. In her experience, Minnie had never been one for lying in. Always a ball of energy, Minnie had often been the first one up in the mornings, bustling around and organising everyone and everything. This new fragile and lethargic Minnie was not the great aunt she knew.

Still, I suppose she is getting old and what with her recent illness and Alice's death, her spirit and body have both taken a battering and need to rest. But a sleep in?

With a sinking heart, Deedee realised that she could not abandon her aunt in her current state of ill health. There was no way she could return to Sydney while her aunt needed her help.

Still, at least that means I have plenty of time to finish those illustrations and maybe do something else.

The rest of the morning passed productively. After putting some soup on to slowly simmer, she headed up the path to Alice's studio full of determination to focus on the work at hand. The day had warmed into a mild spring day. In the sun the warmth was obvious, yet in the shade the chill from the previous night lingered. It came as no surprise that Alice's studio was cool, if not cold. Fortunately, Alice had always been a woman who liked her creature comforts. Deedee, after a bit of a search, located a small fan heater which, once turned on, quickly drove the chill from the small room. After pushing Alice's stuff to one side and creating a space on the long counter, Deedee spread out her paints, brushes and paper. The illustration she had previously been working on was considered and deemed to be satisfactory. Although, a bit more work was required before Deedee would consider it complete. But had she done enough to illustrate this story? She reached into her satchel and pulled out a folder tied shut with a loose string. She took out a stack of papers and laid them out on the table, in order. Deedee stood back and silently contemplated them, before reordering the sheets on which she had painted various illustrations. As if satisfied they were now in the correct order, she nodded and proceeded to examine each image intently. Were they now ready to be shared with the publisher, the author and the designer? She appreciated that these were not the final illustrations—so much more needed to be done before they got to that stage. But did they give sufficient information that she could now proceed to the final draft? The pages of the story she had selected to illustrate made sense to *her*, but she knew there was a strong chance she would receive suggested changes or requests for further illustrations from the publisher, the author and/or the designer. Creating a book was a collaborative exercise, and while at times that could be frustrating when her vision for the illustrations was rejected, sometimes she felt her work benefited from a consultative approach. And today she was focussed on finalising this last illustration prior to scanning and sending all her work to the publisher and designer. She knew there would then be a rush of phone calls and emails as they worked towards the final draft—and further painting would be required. Deedee, knowing only too well that, like all other stories she had worked on, there would be a publishing deadline, so she expected that the pressure would soon be increasing. Already she could sense the publisher's growing anxiety just from the frequency and tone of their emails. Still, she could only do so much each day. In a way, she wondered if the author had the best position in terms of process—their part in it already being done. But they could still have some comments about whether Deedee's illustrations enhanced the story, or if her proposed illustrations accorded with their vision. Some of this had already been clarified in earlier consultations when Deedee shared her initial sketches with the author and the publisher, but she knew from experience how the situation could unexpectedly change, and without notice.

By lunchtime, the final illustration was complete. Leaving it to dry in the studio, Deedee returned to the house to find her aunt up and about, bustling in the kitchen as she fussed over the soup Deedee had put on to cook. Her aunt looked much brighter and, judging by the way she ordered her great-niece around, she was also feeling more like her usual self.

'Ah there you are. I was beginning to wonder if I would see you again today or whether you would be like Alice when she got carried away with her inspiration. You know, shut up in the studio for hours until the lack of light drove her away. I take it things have gone well today?'

'Yes. Really well. I'm happy with the progress. Or maybe that's not the right word. My illustrations are ready to be scanned and sent off to the publisher this afternoon. So, I am at your disposal. What do you want to do this afternoon? Just please tell me it doesn't involve more gardening!'

Minnie, amid ladling soup into two blue and white striped

bowls, looked up at Deedee and snorted, 'Go on. Gardening's good for the soul. And who knows? That young Harry might be back this afternoon. Surely helping him would be fun?'

Deedee smiled. Subtlety was not her aunt's best quality. Still, at least she now knew her aunt was feeling better. If she was well enough to plot a bit of obvious matchmaking, then things couldn't be too bad.

The soup turned out to be much better than Deedee had originally expected. When she had thrown it together that morning, using random ingredients located in the refrigerator, she was apprehensive. With a vague recipe in mind, she had created a sort of minestrone which, once they grated some parmesan cheese on top and sprinkled it generously with chopped parsley, had turned out to be rather tasty. And unlike the other day, the toast had not burned this time. Slathered with melted butter, it was the perfect accompaniment. All in all, not too bad.

With no sign of Harry, it was not too hard to convince Minnie that it was a good idea to go for a drive and maybe stop in for afternoon tea at a nearby winery.

Some time spent sitting in the sunshine tasting local wines and snacking on a cheese plate, they both agreed was a pleasant way to enjoy the spring weather. An outing and some fresh scenery would work wonders with her aunt. Throughout the drive, Minnie was full of chatter—pointing out places of interest, sharing with her great-niece anecdotes regarding various local characters whose properties they were passing. The energy level in the car rose as the stories became more outrageous. Minnie swore that they were totally true and there appeared to be no reason to doubt her.

'Who knew life could be so exciting in this quiet little place? I always thought those TV soapies set in rural communities were totally made up, but after hearing your tales I am not so sure.'

'And I haven't told you the half of it!' chuckled Minnie. Leaning back into the car seat, she breathed an extended sigh of satisfaction. 'Deedee dear, thank you for this outing. I hadn't realised how housebound I have been in recent times. Today has been a treat. It reminds me of those times Alice and I used to cruise the countryside. When her painting had gone well, and I was not wanting to do any more in the garden. On those days we would head out of town in any random direction and go exploring. So many interesting villages and communities nearby—with cafés, wine bars, and did I mention the chocolatier not that far away from where we are now? Sometimes, of course, we would head into Canberra—to see the galleries and the art. I have always been a bit of a philistine, but Alice—well, she would get lost in the artwork, and I would eventually have to drag her away.' This time there was another sigh, but not one of satisfaction, more an echo of the sorrowful memories wafting over Minnie.

Deedee said nothing. She wasn't sure what she could say to ease the moment. Then, as she turned her head to check on her aunt's wellbeing, she noticed a slight smile on Minnie's face and the fluttering of her eyelids. There was no need to speak. She concentrated on the road ahead and left her aunt to her memories, a gentle snore soon audible.

By evening, both Deedee and Minnie were pleasantly weary and agreed to make an early night of it. Lying in her bed, and just before sleep overwhelmed her, Deedee contemplated the success that had been her day. The completion of her paintings, now successfully scanned and sent off to the publisher, felt like the achievement of a major milestone. She realised what a load that obligation had become. Normally, such a job would have been something she would have efficiently whipped through, and without conscious thought. But for some reason, this project had weighed heavy on her. Maybe because it had been interrupted by her aunt's illness and the need to hurry down here, or maybe it was something more. Perhaps it was a sign she no longer wanted to do such work and was ready to try something else. Deedee immediately dismissed that thought. To think of alternatives required far more energy than she could muster. It was best to stick with the safe and known for now. Especially when her aunt needed her. There was only so much change she could take on.

Yet, as she lay in bed and stretched out her stiffening legs, the thought of her random meeting with Julian that morning made her smile. Those long legs, that twinkly smile, the wild hair, and that sense of connection—what was there not to like? With any luck, she might feel more of the same when she saw again him the following day. Her alarm was set, her running gear was laid out, and she was ready to meet him again for a further run in the morning— that was if her legs could manage it.

Chapter Fifteen

Awake before the alarm sounded, Deedee wasted no time getting dressed and heading outside. The pink streaks of dawn, still apparent, were showing through the boundary trees but fading with the imminent arrival of the sun. As Deedee opened the front gate, a shadowy figure emerged from the shadows made by the overhanging greenery.

'Good morning. I wasn't sure if you would be up and about so early, so I was trying to hide and not look like a stalker,' Julian said with a welcoming smile.

'We agreed to meet, didn't we?' said Deedee, trying not to sound too indignant. Of course, she would be here. She'd agreed to it after all. Once again, feeling that electric tingle as she drew closer to him, she knew there was no way she would have not turned up.

With a jerk of her head in the direction of the river path, and a quick jog on the spot, she added, 'Come on. It's too cool to stand still. Let's get going. We can talk as we run.'

'Clearly you are fitter than I am if you can do that! You talk and I'll grunt. That's about all I'm capable of.'

Deedee soon concluded that Julian was exaggerating his unfitness. With her shorter legs, she struggled to keep up with his casual lope. The conversation, such as it was, quickly petered out and all that could be heard was the thud of feet overlaid with intensifying puffing. Until Deedee called a halt.

'Enough! I need to stop and get my breath. You are such a

liar. Not unfit at all, are you? Let me guess. You do triathlons or something. That would explain the trendy gear.'

'Trendy gear? This?' he said while pulling at the logo-enhanced lycra shirt that clung most satisfyingly to his defined chest muscles. 'You forget I live in the inner city. This is essential attire for jogging in Centennial Park. My urban uniform so to speak.'

'And mine? What is mine?' laughed Deedee.

'Well, I would hate to cause offence, but I can only assume you are channelling Northern Beaches hippy chick. It's the only place where you might have street cred in that attire.'

Deedee looked down at her ripped leggings which fortunately were largely covered by a baggy T-shirt, thus preserving an element of modesty. The only thing of value was her new—well, sort of new—running shoes.

'Alright, I give up,' she said holding her hands up in surrender. 'I can't compete with you in the fashion stakes, but I bet I can beat you to the coffee shop. I think my need for coffee is greater than yours!'

'You're on!'

Once again, the coffee shop was full of other caffeine deprived customers who were happy to squeeze up and make room for the two joggers at the long table in the centre of the back room. Enough room was made for them to sit next to each other on a battered wooden bench. They were so close that Deedee's thigh pressed against his and their shoulders jostled for position— especially when they reached for their hot cups of coffee. Deedee tried hard not to react to this closeness and focussed on keeping the conversation flowing. Still, she could not help but be distracted by the warmth of his leg and the clean fresh smell of the man seated so close to her. Fortunately, Julian was in full flow and spoke at length about the real reason why he was lingering in town.

'You see I am trying to convince my father that we need to develop the land next to your great-aunt's place. The town is screaming out for more residential land and those paddocks would be perfect. With my project management training, I could co-ordinate everything.'

With a sinking feeling, she contemplated the impact of Julian's words. Residential development, and next to Minnie's house. Then, the significance of what he was saying really registered.

'Was it you then? Are you the person that has been snooping around Minnie's home? Creeping up on her in the garden, frightening her and the others?'

'The others? I don't know what you mean. I only saw your aunt. And I definitely don't creep!' Julian held up his hand before Deedee, in obvious indignation, could say anything.

'Yes, I did speak to your aunt and if I frightened her, I am sorry. I'm told I can be seen as intimidating because of my height, but that certainly was not my intention. I was merely wanting to see if she was interested in selling. Her block would provide excellent access to our development—off the main road and all.'

As Deedee struggled to consider the meaning of what he was saying, the true significance quickly dawned.

'Access? But there is a house there. Surely you don't mean demolishing the house to create a road … surely not?' she added in dawning horror.

Speaking slowly, as if talking to someone who was slow on the uptake which, maybe because she felt shocked, she was—or could it be that what he was saying was beyond her comprehension—Julian added, 'It's an old house. A dump really. Anyone can see that it is falling down. A few more years and it will be beyond saving. It's an old worker's cottage, not a mansion or anything historic, and it won't be missed if it's gone. Think about it—using that land would provide perfect access for the new development. We could line the roadway with trees that mirror those along the river. Perhaps include some picnic benches. And maybe we could call the access road after your great-aunt—we could call it *Minnie's Lane*. Now wouldn't that be something?' Julian leaned forward to grasp his coffee cup, a complacent grin on his face as if he was sure he had convinced his listener with his unassailable logic. But he hadn't.

'But it's our home. It's been a home for so many generations. You can feel their presence still—in the woodwork and in the garden.'

Literally she thought but decided not to add any further clarification. 'The history of this town is bound up in the very timber and brick of our house. It tells the story of the settlement here and for that reason it has links to more than just me and Minnie.'

Julian huffed. Clearly sentimentality was not going to appeal to him.

'If it is so important, turn it into a museum. Anyway, if you and your aunt don't do something very soon, it will be a pile of rubble—whether you sell to us or not. Anyone can see it is hanging on by a thread and your old aunt is no better. Deedee, you really do need to be realistic. Your aunt and that house are both as dangerous as each other. It's a wonder the council hasn't taken steps to have it condemned. I guess there is still some goodwill regarding your aunt, and maybe they are waiting until she passes. And from the look of her when I saw her in the garden the other day, that won't be too long.'

The pressure of Julian's thigh against hers no longer felt enticing, or like an invitation for further contact. It had morphed into a threat, a hint of what could come if his will were to dominate hers. But what he said made sense. The house was rapidly deteriorating—just like her aunt—and at this stage, Deedee was at a loss as to what to do. While her brain could appreciate the logic of his comments, there was no way she would be party to her beloved childhood home and refuge being condemned to destruction, like it was a useless relic. Carefully, she eased herself off the bench, smiling her thanks at the neighbouring stranger who made way for her. There seemed no point in continuing any conversation with Julian.

'Julian, I had best go. There's really no reason for us to keep on with this discussion. I'm now not sure why you made the effort to get to know me. Was it because you saw getting close to me as a way of convincing my aunt to sell?' She saw a surging flare of anger in his eyes before it was shut down and replaced by a neutrally controlled expression. Deedee continued, holding up her hand as if gesturing him to stop.

'No. Don't say anything more. I think you've said enough. Let's leave it for now. Your motives are clear, and I see no reason why we should prolong our contact or speak further—on this matter, or any other matter. I would be lying if I said I wished you well. I'm just disappointed you thought you could use me in this manner. Goodbye.'

Deedee turned and left the café. It wasn't until she was two blocks down the road and turning into the street for home that she realised she hadn't paid for her coffee. *Oh, well, let him pay for it. Or I might have to check in with them tomorrow. But there's no way I'm going back there today. Or going jogging tomorrow for that matter. At least my muscles will thank me for that!*

A different young woman returned to the garden, so different to the one that had left not too much earlier that morning. While it seemed so much longer, she knew that only a little over an hour had elapsed since she had bounced out of bed and rushed to meet the person who seemed to offer so much promise. It had soon become clear that whatever he was promising came at a price, and not one she was prepared to pay. The angst about whether she was prepared to give up her life in Sydney and return to her childhood home to care for her aunt, had disappeared in an instant. It dissipated as soon as Julian made it clear that he held contempt for her home, and that his intent was to turn it into a paved asphalted road. The anger his words had invoked had propelled her out of the café and back down the road, but now as she pushed open the side gate, it was replaced with a rush of sorrow. *How could anyone want to destroy such beauty* she thought as she gazed at the garden in the full flush of its spring glory. *What was with such people?*

'Penny for them?' A voice intruded her thoughts. She looked up and there, in the middle of the nearest garden bed, secateurs in hand, was Harry.

'I thought I'd make an early start on it,' he explained, as if feeling the need to justify his presence so early in the morning. 'Finish the pruning then see what Madam had in mind to be done to the front verandah. Seems to me I need to do a complete rebuild but she may think otherwise.'

He took a closer look at Deedee. Not liking what he saw, he

closed the secateurs, replaced them in his pocket and moved out of the bed, taking care not to tread on the plants. Even though she was feeling upset, some part of Deedee's mind still registered the care he was taking.

I like that. Unlike that other man, he is not in the business of destruction. She smiled at him in a watery manner, tears threatening, but she held back for now—just.

Deedee sighed, unsure how she could explain what had just occurred in a way that didn't divulge the tentative hopes she had been harbouring about that man. There was no need to name him anymore. *That man* was all she would call him from now on.

'It's quite a story and I really don't want to drag you away from your work. But I suppose you could say I've had a bit of a shock this morning.'

An arm, a comforting arm, took hers and led her to a nearby bench.

'Come on. Tell Uncle Harry. I've had experience of looking after you in the past, so I reckon I can do it again—if you need me to that is. Go on, spit it out.'

In a halting manner, Deedee told Harry about her recent contact with Julian. Harry frowned, wrinkling his forehead in concern, but he did not interrupt. When she outlined her dismay about discovering his intentions for Minnie's house, Harry's anger erupted.

'That does it! I knew something was up but hadn't realised exactly what. That family is way too much. They really don't need your aunt's place for road access to any development—assuming the council would ever approve it—they just want to have a grand entrance off the main road and don't care how they achieve it. Even if it means frightening a little old lady, they will stop at nothing that family! Believe me, I know. All they think of is themselves.' Harry drew a breath and visibly tried to calm himself. 'I'm sorry Deedee that you had to endure his weasel words. I hope you sent him on his way. In fact, I'm sure you are more than a match for him!'

With a laugh Deedee realised she was and that she had been spared even more hurt. Imagine if she had allowed the relationship, such as it was, to progress. There could have been heartbreak for sure. After all, she now had good reason to suspect that Julian's motives in encouraging his connection with her, were not so pure. Even as she sat there half listening to Harry's soothing words, and trying to accept that Julian was bad news, there was still a part of her that wondered if a bit more contact with Julian might have been worthwhile. The feeling of electricity between them—that thigh pressed against hers—had hinted at the potential for a fiery encounter. Now she would never know.

Chapter Sixteen

Leaving Harry to his labours, a calmer Deedee headed inside. *What was it about sharing one's troubles that made it so much better?* she wondered. It's not like the situation had changed. Julian had still been an arse, but somehow, once she had been able to share the story with another, her feelings of woe had lessened. She no longer felt the need to cry, but instead she felt concerned that she had been a fool, falling for a magnetic personality and entrapped like an insect in a spider's web. It was a lucky escape she told herself. But still ...

She found Minnie in the kitchen, bent over as she pulled containers out of an open cupboard with noisy determination. Merlin sat nearby in a patch of sunlight, once again preoccupied with his endless grooming, only acknowledging her entry by a flicker of his ears.

Minnie must be feeling much better, Deedee thought with a smile. This was the Minnie that she was used to—a pocket dynamo in perpetual motion.

'What ARE you up to?' Deedee asked, having to repeat herself to be heard over the racket of containers being thrown onto the wooden floor.

Minnie leaned back and peered up at her niece.

'Ah, there you are my dear. And a good morning to you. I see you have been up and about. Well done you. It's good to be busy and therefore I decided this morning that busy is what I must be. So, I have set myself a list of tasks. First thing is to order this mess in the kitchen. Then that Harry and I are going to agree on what needs doing to the verandah. Once we do that, I'll leave him to it and then go onto the task I've been putting off for ages.'

'Ages? If you've been putting it off, it must be a big job. Do you need any help?'

'No dear. I must do this on my own. It's time I sorted out the mess in this house and in particular, deal with Alice's possessions. I haven't done it until now as it seemed so final—like truly saying goodbye to Alice. But somehow my recent turn has got me thinking. What is left of Alice are the memories and her stuff—heaps of stuff I might add. The memories I will have with me forever, sparing the onset of dementia that is. But Alice's belongings, well they are merely objects—things that are no longer of any use to her—or me for that matter. But they could be of use to others who may have the greater need. I think that is what she would want me to do—use her stuff to help others. So, once I have sorted the kitchen out, I will attack Alice's wardrobe and work out what can go to the charity shop.'

Minnie gazed at her great-niece. 'No, don't even offer. I don't need your help. Thank you all the same. I feel like this is private time between me and Alice. You go off and find something to do. At some stage you can help me with her studio. There must be some equipment up there that you will need. I can somehow sense Alice's presence up in her little studio, so for that reason I might need you there with me. Not for moral support, but I think more as a way to be together when we bid Alice a final goodbye.'

With a resolute expression and her lips tightly closed, Minnie turned away from her niece and once again peered into the dusty cupboard. Even in grief, Minnie was determined not to show any sign that could be interpreted as weakness.

Leaving her aunt to it, Deedee wandered outside back into the garden, sketchbook and pencils in hand. An idea was forming. Perhaps it was because of the threat of demolition that Julian had raised in their conversation that morning, or maybe it was due to the realisation of her aunt's increasing frailty and the imminent changes associated with that, but for some reason Deedee felt a growing need to preserve the image of the cottage and the garden as a way of honouring all those who had lived within its sheltering walls. It could be a series of vignettes that captured the lives lived here. Maybe an image of Bertie in his empire, Alice and her studio, and Minnie up to her elbows weeding in a garden bed. But where should she be? On the verandah perhaps—where she once sat when she was young. Maybe the child Deedee escaping from those endless chores, hiding with her head in a book, heedless to those demanding calls from Minnie and Alice.

She would gift this work to Minnie as a way of saying thank you for taking her in, giving her a home and a shaping her future all those years ago. Minnie always spoke of memories being something she treasured. Hopefully, her artwork would invoke those cherished memories.

Striding down the curved stone path, she headed towards the enormous elm tree which she now knew was Bertie's empire. With a bit of luck, and if she emptied her mind of all distractions, she might come to sense his presence. If not, then she could sketch that part of the garden and use her imagination and memory to create an image of that waiflike child.

Settling on the bench by the table, sketchbook open in front of her, Deedee gazed around as she tried to decide from which angle to draw this part of the garden. The trouble was that from every angle, it looked perfect. Looking back towards the house she could see the path curving around garden beds, bursting with growth and massed colour. In the background, the pitched roof of the house was clearly visible punctuated by two chimneys. The actual body of the house, more a shadow behind the vegetation, added depth to the scene, but it was not clearly identifiable as a defined structure. But if she drew that aspect, she would not be able to include the massive elm that dominated this part of the garden which, by its very size and untrimmed branches, added a dimension of wildness to this part of the garden. She nodded to herself. It definitely needed to be included—that tree and Bertie seemed to belong to each other. She turned on the bench, faced the tree and took a moment to appreciate the completely different display before her. So close to her, the mottled and gnarled trunk dominated the scene. The random stone path below that curved around the trunk was twisted and buckled, having been reshaped over the decades by tree roots as they pushed upwards with expanded growth. A stray blackbird scratched in the leaf litter and then paused, cocking its head as it considered the stranger at the bench who was now quickly sketching, capturing its essence in a few calculated lines. With a chatter of alarm, the bird flew away when the bushes near the tree rustled. But there was no wind blowing to disturb those bushes. Deedee paused in her sketching and willed herself to remain still. Could this be the boy returning? There was a glimmer and a hint of shape as the familiar face of a young boy emerged from the bushes, his body gradually becoming apparent. The same faded blue shirt, little more than a rag and the patched trousers held together with string. The shape drifted closer. Judging by the smile on his face, Deedee had been recognised, her presence in his territory welcome.

'It's you Missus Deedee. Where have you been? I've been waiting for you.'

'Sorry Bertie. I've been busy, but I'm here now and I want to do some drawings of the garden—and maybe you if you'll let me.'

'Me? Draw me? Missus, no one has ever asked to draw me! Little Bert? In a picture? That would be an honour. I can pose anyway and anywhere you like,' he said while striking a number of what he clearly considered to be heroic poses—hands on both hips, arms posed as if shooting a bow and arrow, or as if flexing his muscles.

Deedee smiled. Little boys, even ghost little boys, still want to play at being the hero.

'Just be yourself Bertie. I want to draw you just as you are, and with that lovely smile. And of course, with your tree. Perhaps you could show me your favourite place by the tree.'

Bert nodded and took up a position in a spot by the base of the tree, sitting in a boy-sized depression between two protruding roots and leaning back stared directly at Deedee.

'Will this do Missus?' he said while clasping his hands around his knees.

'Perfect. Now stay very still and I will be as quick as I can.' Deedee started to sketch and then paused, another image forming in her mind. The image of Bert all those years ago, carving a small bird for a desolate young girl who had lost everything and everyone that had been dear to her.

'You know what Bertie? We might try another pose. Do you still like to carve?'

At his nod, Deedee continued, 'Perhaps if you could look like you were concentrating on carving something, I might try to sketch that.'

'Better than that Missus Deedee, I'll carve you another bird.' And as if by magic, another half-carved piece of wood materialised in his hand. Bertie bent his head forward, and with a battered pocketknife in hand, he focussed on the task at hand, all the while whistling the same mysterious tune that Deedee had heard so many times before.

Deedee's fingers flew. Ghost or no ghost, she knew little boys did not sit still for long. The image in her mind that she wanted to capture included the ghost child before her, leaning into the sheltering tree and concentrating on the bird he was carving. Yet, she also wanted to include in her sketch the bird she saw scratching in the leaf litter not that long ago. A bird, that if she positioned it correctly in the sketch, would form the inspiration for the boy's carving. If she was successful, the resulting picture would, she hoped, evoke the serenity and life that was present in this garden.

Deedee was so focussed on the sketching that it was some time before she became aware that the tuneless whistling had ceased. She looked up and realised that her companion was no longer with her.

Drat that boy! Still, I've pretty much got all I need for this picture, she thought as she considered her sketch.

An approaching tuneless whistle could be heard heading towards her from down the path. It was a bit louder than what she had heard earlier—full of energy and more alive. It had to be Harry, and sure enough it was.

'I came looking for you. I figured you would be here somewhere. Time for a break. I have the coffee, the cake and two mugs. Fancy joining me?'

Deedee's nod was sufficient.

'This way then. Bring your stuff. You don't want to leave it here for our friend to steal. Come on. I think morning tea on the front verandah is the place to be. Let's avoid anywhere near your aunt. I heard a lot of swearing and clattering a little while ago. I went and peeped in. She didn't see me, thank goodness. There she was in the kitchen trying to sort out every plastic container known to man, and she was making a heavy go of it too. We should leave her be … for quite a while I suspect.'

As they drank their coffee and ate slices of another excellent cake baked by Harry's mother—chocolate this time—Deedee explained what she had been doing.

'A series of sketches—snapshots I suppose—that speak of the lives lived in this house and garden. So, in keeping with the rustic theme, I'm keeping them simple. I'll do pencil sketches then I'll colour them using my watercolour paints. It's a technique I've often used to illustrate children's books. I get a beautiful line with the pencil work and the watercolours bring it to life—but with a quaint, old-fashioned feel. A bit like this house and garden. See, I've done this one already this morning.' Deedee spread out the sketchbook where the almost completed picture of Bertie and bird was displayed.

'That's amazing. You've captured the mischief of our young friend and his creativity. I can almost hear him whistling. You've got the expression just right. Did he pose for you?'

'For a little while, until he lost interest and faded away. And what is it with you and Bertie and that whistling? It's the same tune. What is it?'

'I have no idea.' Harry shook his head as if to clear the cobwebs in his brain. 'It's funny, but I think I must have picked it up from him. I often sense and hear him in this garden. Always have, now

I come to think of it—since I was a little boy. I must have learned that tune from him. No idea what it is. Some historian might be able to tell us. But you know what?' Harry glanced at her and said with a gentle smile, 'The funny thing is, I only ever seem to whistle that tune when I am here in this garden. When I work at other locations, I turn the radio on. Somehow it seems wrong to do that here. Modern music doesn't seem appropriate for this setting. Anyway, it is a treat to hear the birdsong and not have it drowned out by the music of the 21st century.'

He started to gather the now empty mugs and cake container.

'Well, that's it for me now. Back to work. What are you doing next?'

'I'm going to sketch my childhood self sitting on this cane chair on the verandah, head in a book and lost to the world.'

'Lost to the world you may have been, but I bet you had the same company then as we have now. Look carefully behind you. Very carefully and no sudden moves.'

As Deedee half turned, as if peering into another part of the garden, she glanced from the corner of her eye towards the parlour window. There on the windowsill sat a glossy black cat—no surprises there—but in the murky gloom behind him she could discern two faces staring right at her. They had shawls wrapped around their shoulders, hair tightly scraped into buns on top of their heads, both sporting disapproving expressions.

'See?' said Harry. 'You're never alone in this place!'

Chapter Seventeen

The sudden burst of energy that had propelled Minnie into kitchen reorganisation mode had filled her with optimism.

I must be feeling better if I can bring myself to face this mess, she told herself as she considered the chaos of kitchen equipment now spread across the kitchen floor. By her calculation, neither she nor Alice had ever reorganised the kitchen in the decades they had lived here. She found herself wondering why she had even thought this was a good idea. So many plastic lids that had no matching containers. Well at least the partnerless lids and containers could go into the recycling where, with a bit of luck, they might be rebirthed into something more useful. Not a happy thought she concluded. No recycling for her. Her perfect match now gone, there was little prospect of being recycled into another partnership, even if she had wanted one.

Her needs were few. She no longer required so much kitchen equipment. Even with Deedee here, their cooking remained basic, and it was not like she entertained anymore. It was time to get ruthless.

It didn't take long to separate those items destined for recycling from those to go to the charity shop. Minnie stacked the overflowing cardboard boxes just inside the back door for Harry to deal with and returned to the kitchen. The mostly empty cupboards greeted her, displaying more spare space than they had for years.

Not bad she thought. Why did I need all this stuff anyway?

Turning to the pantry and faced with the prospect of sorting through shelves of items past their 'use by' dates, her energy suddenly deserted her.

Mustn't rush things. Maybe that's enough for today. There's only so much tidying up one old woman can do.

The old chair by the fire seemed to call out to her. Merlin, wandering into the room from up the corridor, gazed at her inscrutably and sat on the hearth before settling into rest that resembled that of someone who had been working hard.

Now what have you been up to Merlin my lad? wondered Minnie as she leaned into the chair and relaxed into a well-earned snooze.

Chapter Eighteen

There was no way Deedee was going to forget her planned outing with Harry that Saturday. Judging by the frequent reminders she had received—both by text and whenever she came across him in the garden, she sensed Harry might be feeling rather anxious that she might pull out of the commitment. Even Minnie was in on the game, asking her what she would be wearing and what time Harry would be picking her up.

'Aunt. Don't fuss. It's not like it is a visit to royalty. I'll just wear what I always wear—jeans and a shirt. Or do I need my hat and gloves?'

'No need to be quite so uppity young lady,' Minnie said, softening the impact of her words with a smile and a quick hug. 'I'm just pleased you are finally getting to meet Harry's mother. She was once friendly with your mum you know, and they do live in a heavenly location. You'll see.'

'Do you want to come with us?' Deedee asked as the thought occurred to her that by going out on her own, she was excluding her aunt from a pleasurable treat.

Minnie shook her head. 'No, not at all. But maybe next time. I haven't been there for years. Not since your mum was visiting us and we would both go out to the farm together. There are quite a few memories out there for me, so let's leave it for now. When I'm feeling a bit stronger and you are confident you know the way to the farm, then I think I could possibly go and brave that road again.

Mind you, once you see the road, you may only want to visit once. I seem to recall that road being quite the challenge. While a lot of things have changed over the years in this community, I'm sure that dirt road isn't one of them!'

Minnie's words replayed in Deedee's mind several days later as she hung on tightly trying to maintain her seat with each jarring jolt as the ute hit what seemed to be an endless procession of potholes.

'Sorry about the road. It's a bit bad at the moment,' Harry said as they traversed a particularly jarring stretch of the road.

'Understatement that,' she replied, clutching the hand strap that hung from the car roof. 'Is it always as bad as this?'

'Probably. In fact, it gets much worse when it rains. Sometimes, after heavy rain, the dirt road is so boggy we can't get out and have to wait for it to dry out.'

'Why doesn't the council do anything?'

'They have better things to do with their money. There's only a few of us who live down this road, so it is not the best use of the council funds to seal it. The best we can hope for is that they grade it a couple of times a year. Invariably, as soon as the road is graded and the potholes smoothed over, it rains, and the road is washed out all over again. I reckon the best way to bring on the rain is to repair the dirt road—seems to work every time!'

Although Harry had indicated his family lived just a 'little way out of town', the drive seemed to take a good half hour. After leaving town, they headed along a sealed road for some time, first passing the outskirts of the town populated with neat suburban houses, then small acreages—the domain of hobby farmers. Small holdings were awash with ponies and horses, all rugged up against the still chilly spring air. Further on, the holdings expanded in size. Paddocks became larger and buildings fewer. The animals of choice in these paddocks mostly sheep or cattle.

Deedee gazed around in wonder at the animals and the expanses of rolling grasslands here and there, dotted with ancient gum trees.

'You know, in all the years I lived here with Minnie and Alice, I have never been out on this road. I suppose they were both city folk originally, so we made our fun in town or if we went anywhere, it was usually a trip to Canberra. But this is amazing. Such a landscape.'

'Wait 'til you see the farm,' Harry said complacently, as if it was the best place on earth. And maybe in his opinion it was. 'Still, we've got a little way further to go. Not too far, just a bit of a dirt road.'

After ten minutes on said dirt road, and with their destination still nowhere in sight, Deedee spluttered, 'A bit of a dirt road? A bit, you said.'

'You get used to it. It's worth it, you'll see,' he said as he shifted the gear stick into a lower gear. 'Here we go. One more grid and we are on our place.'

They rattled over another cattle grid. Alongside it was a large sign with oversized letters, impossible to miss. **SWEETWATER** – *Private Property. Trespassers will be Prosecuted.*

Not very welcoming, Deedee thought. *But maybe that is the way in the country. Say it as it is. No room for ambiguity.*

The dirt road traversed several more paddocks populated with sheep and fat lambs before they turned and headed up what was clearly a driveway. No native gums in this house yard. European deciduous trees, now in the first leaf of spring, lined the drive. Dotted around the house yard were other specimen trees and close to the house was a large pond with an ornamental fountain. The house was a sprawling, single-storey construction of indeterminate age, largely screened from view by the wide verandahs that offered shelter from the elements. Judging by the collection of worn chairs and sofas grouped in hospitable clusters at various locations along their length, it was evident that these verandahs were well used.

'Is this garden all your work?' Deedee asked as she gazed around, taking in the formal design of the landscaping, a marked contrast to the casual, wild beauty of Minnie's garden.

'Not really. I keep it tidy for Mum, but it is more her design. A bit too *landed gentry* for me! I'm more the casual type,' he said, smiling across at Deedee as he slowed the car to a halt on the gravel driveway.

Deedee, taking in Harry's casual attire of threadbare checked flannelette shirt and frayed jeans, could only agree with him.

'Yes, I think you might be right. I can't see you as a black tie and tails sort of man.'

'You might be surprised. I could be a man of hidden depths. If you are still around when we hold our spring ball, I will take you and you will see a new man.'

How could she possibly refuse? Looking at Harry's smiling face and twinkling eyes, Deedee found herself, without conscious thought, agreeing to his invitation.

'You're on. A hot date at a spring ball with a scrubbed-up man that I probably won't recognise. Of course, I'll be there. And who knows I might surprise you when you see the new me!'

'Hah! Come on. No time for chitchat. I need to introduce you to Mum and then I'll take you on a tour of the place. When I left this morning, Mum was cooking another of her famous cakes in your honour. It should be done by now. You know, I should bring you out here every Saturday. That way I would be sure of getting decent cake.'

'Do you only think of your stomach?'

'Pretty much. Doesn't everyone?'

It was clear good humour ran in this family, as did good looks. Harry's mother provided a warm welcome in a no fuss way.

'Just call me Sarah dear, none of that Mrs Frost rubbish,' she said as she greeted Deedee with a quick hug and a kiss on the cheek. A tall woman of capable bearing, and with eye-crinkled good humour etched onto her face, she smiled her welcome. 'Now let me get a good look at you,' she said while stepping back, still holding onto Deedee with both her hands.

Deedee submitted to this examination with as much good grace as she could muster, feeling somewhat like an insect under the microscope.

The inspection did not last long. Whatever Harry's mother had observed, it was apparently to her satisfaction. Leading Deedee into the kitchen, she continued with her patter.

'I haven't seen you since you were a young one—probably about four or five years of age. Your mum and I go way back, and she would often pop out to see me when she was visiting Minnie, or I would head into town to catch up. I can still see the little girl in you—same dark curly hair, those beautiful liquid eyes, and that skin. How lucky you are not to burn in our dreadful sun. I know you have your father's colouring, but there is so much of your mum in you. Now don't shake your head, it's true, believe me. I'll search out some old photos while Harry is showing you the farm and you'll see what I mean.'

Turning to Harry, she continued, 'Morning tea now or later?'

'Both!'

'Go on with you! Anyone would think you were still growing the amount you eat. If you show Deedee around that will give me time to ice the cake and maybe by then the boys will be back.'

'The boys?' Deedee asked, puzzled that there could also be young boys here.

'She means Dad and my brother, Lachie. They'll be out in a paddock somewhere checking stock, fixing the water line or a fence, or whatever today's chore is. Come on, let's get out of Mum's hair so she can focus on that icing.'

They headed to the garage behind the house where a strange four-wheeled vehicle was parked. It had an open canopy with two front seats, and room in the back for the detritus that is a farmer's lot—it was clearly a workhorse.

Harry's dog, Scruff, released from a nearby dog enclosure and after giving a cursory greeting to both humans, leaped into the back of the vehicle. Scruff knew better than to waste time on unimportant social interaction when the opportunity of an outing called.

'What is this vehicle?' Deedee asked as Harry focussed on reversing into a turning bay, and heading out along a back driveway, and back towards the dirt road they had recently traversed which, she now realised, bisected the farm.

'It's our farm vehicle—a type of all-terrain vehicle—we use these every day except when we need to get into the rough stuff, then we use the trail bike or one of the horses, or even—heaven forbid—we actually have to walk! You can see there's room in the back for the dog, or dogs, and any fencing or farm equipment we might think we need to take along with us. It's not a highway vehicle, but certainly a great thing to have here on the farm. Now, I'm just going to give you a bit of a guided tour and then I want to show you something special.'

To the backdrop of Harry's rambling commentary, Deedee found herself listening with one ear while she gazed around her with wonder. She realised that the road traversing the farm was heading down the middle of a valley that gently sloped to a wide, slowly flowing, river. Now she had her bearings, well sort of, Deedee realised that this expanse of water was the Murrumbidgee—the big river that had its headwaters in the Snowy Mountains and skirted many communities, large and small, on its way downstream. While she had, in theory, understood this river was nearby, it had never featured in her life until now. Gazing at its beauty, she wondered why not.

'The river's pretty full at the moment. We've had some good rain over winter. Sometimes, in summer, the river barely flows. It can get so low that the sand flats become exposed and the cattle try to cross. You know, something about the grass on the other side being greener. Not that it always is. Nor can they get too far. You can see the rocky hills on the other side are a bit of a disincentive to wander. They usually return, sometimes with a few buddies they've found on the other side. Makes for interesting conversations with our neighbours!'

Harry made for a good tour guide. Not only could he speak with authority about the farm, but he also took great care to share with her his knowledge of the landscape—the trees, the wildlife and the nature of the rocky crags that were visible on the eroded hills.

'This is limestone country, full of fossils too. From a time when it must have been part of an inland sea. Thinking about that makes me feel rather insignificant and realise that many of my worries are of no concern in the overall scheme of things. And this vista helps too. Seeing this beauty every day—the changing colours with the seasons, and the time of day, can't help but soothe my soul.'

'Wow Harry. That's deep. I didn't know you had it in you?'

'I told you, a man of hidden depths. Still, living here maybe you can understand why the big city wouldn't cut it for me. Listen.'

With that he turned off the engine and held up his hand to his ear in a command to pay attention and listen.

And they did. The universe settled, as the world around them resumed its everyday life and paid them no mind. Deedee was conscious of a gentle breeze tickling her cheek and fluttering her curls. She lifted her head and smelled—nearby scents of animal manure mingling with the distinctive tangy fragrance from the eucalyptus trees that lined the fences. The sounds, growing in complexity the more she paid attention—a magpie call from an adjacent tree, its melodious watery gurgle competing with the bleating from lambs in the next paddock. In the distance, the chug from a tractor, and even further away a bark from one of the farm dogs that they had left incarcerated in the dog run behind the house. But other than that, silence—none of the sounds that had formed her previous existence in the city. No constant hum of traffic, no screeching of tyres, no honking of horns, or noise from overhead aircraft. With the absence of such sounds, Deedee realised how they had impacted on her subconscious, creating an underlying awareness of constant movement and action. Here there was none of that. The world before her was silent—by and large. Such sounds as she could hear, were intermittent. It required all of her attention to notice them. The screech of the cockatoo as it flew over, gone almost as soon as it registered. A flutter and a squawk from a flock of parrots as they passed overhead. Harry registered their presence and commented.

'They're heading for the river, watch them. They'll perch in the casuarina trees that line the river, find some tucker, and maybe get a drink. I love watching them swoop by—a flash of colour and then they're gone.' With a shake of his head, Harry leaned forward and once again started the engine. 'That's enough poetry for you, I want to show you something. I've got an idea and I hope you can help me.' At Deedee's look of inquiry, Harry laughed. 'No, not yet. I'll explain in a minute. Just relax and enjoy the drive—if you can.'

She soon understood what Harry meant as he turned the vehicle and headed upwards following a sort of track that led to the top of a nearby hill. Not too steep, but steep enough that she felt the need to hold on tight as they were jolted to and fro while traversing the rough and washed-out terrain. Once they stopped however, she decided the discomfort was worth it. The vista stretching out before her was breathtaking.

Harry had stopped the vehicle on a level area at the top of a craggy rise that looked down onto the farm and across the river towards the serried hills stretching as far as the eye could see.

'It's not bad, is it?' Harry said as he gave her a helping hand out of the truck.

'It's more than that,' Deedee exclaimed. 'So high. Like we're on top of the world. And the farm stretched out below like some miniature child's toy.' She took a breath and considered all that was laid out before her, but this time with an artist's eye. 'You know, this scene before us is a lesson in contrasts. The ordered and soft vista of the farm below—soft greens of the pasture all laid out in a methodical manner, almost like a patchwork. See those straight lines of fences and the rectangular shape of the paddocks? Then the river curving along its boundaries and behind it the wilderness. Those rocky hills rising as soon as we look beyond the river—no green there—just brown, ochre and the taupe of rock and dirt punctuated by the olive green of a stunted gum tree. It's amazing!'

'Now, who's being poetic then?' Harry said, poking Deedee with his elbow.

'A view like this deserves it. Yet, there's something strangely familiar about it. Like I've seen it before.'

'Maybe you have. Think on it,' urged Harry, looking at her intently.

With a grimace, she struggled to recall a scene like the one on display before her. And then it came to her. Of course, the half-finished painting in Alice's studio was this exact scene. But why?'

'Alice's painting?' she asked.

'Yep. She was doing it as a favour for me, but sadly it was never finished. That's what my idea was about—you know, the one I mentioned earlier?'

She didn't have a clue what Harry meant and waited for him

to add more. It seemed to be taking a while as Harry stood still, seemingly lost in contemplation of the view before him. He remained silent.

'And?'

He turned to her as if being dragged away from a very deep meditation.

'Mmm? Yes? Sorry, I forgot to tell you. I had asked Alice to paint me the farm as a present for the folks, mainly for Mum really—a sort of special present as I know how much the farm means to them and all. We agreed that the painting should be of this vista. It really captures everything that is magic about this place. but, sadly, she never completed it. And to be honest, it kinda slipped my mind. I suppose I just assumed it wasn't to be. Then when we were in the studio the other day—well, I saw what she had done. It's a magnificent painting, but incomplete. But it got me thinking. I don't suppose you could finish Alice's work, could you?'

At Deedee's look of horror, he stepped back, hands open in a gesture of surrender.

'I thought not. I get it that an artist would not fiddle with another artist's work. So maybe Plan B then?'

'Plan B?'

'Yeah. You also paint this scene or somewhere nearby. That way we could hang them together and they would tell of the evolution of an artwork. In fact, I think Mum and Dad would really like that. Not only because they were very fond of Alice, but it would also speak of change, which is what is constantly happening to the land below us. It is changing with every season and according to how the land is used. If you agree, I can bring you back up here some other time so you can do sketches, or take photos, or whatever you artists do. Agree? Is it a plan?'

Deedee took her time to speak as she tried to make sense of the thoughts swirling in her head. Intuitively there seemed to be no problem in painting the same scene as Alice. Yet, such a sweeping vista could not be captured on a small canvas. It demanded a canvas of significant size so that the immensity before her could be given the treatment it deserved. But she could sense that this might be a challenge too far. Up until now she had always been a creature of confined spaces. A dainty illustration setting off several lines of a child's story did not prepare her for this. Even the sketches she was currently doing of the garden were like the garden itself—small, complex, and exquisitely detailed. Was she prepared to take on this task and risk opening herself up to comparison with Alice? By hanging the two works together, comparison was inevitable. Was she brave enough? At the most basic level, did she even have sufficient skills do it?

As if sensing her uncertainty, Harry added, 'Go on. You can do it. What have you got to lose?'

His encouraging smile tipped the scales, and a decision was reached.

'Alright, I'll do it. But I make no promises. It could end up looking like an illustration from a children's story, with parrots and a wedgetail hovering above and maybe a bunyip or two.'

'Now you're talking! A completely different reinterpretation of the same view—what's not to like? But we'd better get back home. I don't know about you, but all this artistic appreciation is hungry work.'

Chapter Nineteen

Morning tea back at the farm was everything that had been promised. Scones fresh from the oven—crispy and crunchy on the outside yet, when split open, sweetly doughy on the inside. They were delicious when spread with homemade apricot jam and freshly whipped cream, or equally delicious when spread with butter that melted into the still warm scone and dripped onto fingers that just begged to be licked. There was also cake for those who still had room—some sort of iced orange cake by the looks of it—but it was of no interest to Deedee, who focussed on eating the scones, a treat from her childhood. While thoughts of delicious scones prepared by Alice still lingered in her memory, she was pretty sure they had been nowhere as good as these.

'Sarah, these are amazing. Thank you so much for going to all this trouble. I really appreciate it,' Deedee said as she spread butter on what she promised herself would be the last scone.

'You are welcome my dear. It is such a treat to see you after all these years. Last time I saw you, you were still a little girl—all legs, fly away hair, and scabbed knees if I recall correctly.'

'Scabbed knees?' Harry looked at her quizzically.

'Yeah, even then I was a clumsy child. Those trees in Minnie's garden were just made for climbing. It's a wonder I didn't break any bones.'

Harry's mum walked to a side table and returned carrying a battered and bulging photo album.

'While you were out with Harry, I did a bit of searching and found this old album. I thought you might like to see some photos of your mum, and I think there might even be some of your father and you as a little one. Now we'll have to be careful as the album has seen better days and is rather fragile. But if I make a space on the table and we open it carefully, I'm pretty sure we will find something.'

And they did. With each photo unearthed and examined, Deedee could feel her emotions swell. As Sarah exclaimed over images of herself and a young Maggie—Deedee's mum—Deedee could feel her chest growing tighter as she struggled to keep her feelings in check. In the end it had to be said.

'I'm sorry Sarah, but I'm feeling a bit overwhelmed. You see, I've so few photos of my mum and dad and hardly any memories of them. It's hard to explain, but seeing these photos makes me realise how much I have lost. You know, it's like there is a big black hole in me where memories of my early life and my family should have been.'

The tears that had been threatening overwhelmed her. Sarah reached for the box of tissues and with a comforting arm, pulled the now sobbing young woman close.

'There, there my dear. I was being so thoughtless. I just wanted to share with you these photos and didn't give any thought to how it might affect you. Let's take it slowly then. There's just one photo I want to give you today and maybe next time you visit you can look at the photo album on your own. But here, take this one.'

With trembling hands Deedee took the proffered photo and examined it through tear misted eyes. She saw an image of a much younger Deedee—two or three years at most—in the arms of her father who was laughing at something the person taking the photo had just said. Her mother was leaning in, fussing over Deedee, pulling down a hat on her head while Deedee, judging by the scowl on her face, objected to such attention and with two chubby hands, was reaching to pull the hat off. A battle of the wills and it looked like Deedee was losing.

'I never did like wearing hats. I still don't,' she smiled. 'Thank you. Are you sure I can have this?'

'Of course. It's such a happy shot—well, apart from you that is. But you can see how loved you were and how happy your parents were. You know, your mum and I did our nursing training together?'

'No, I didn't. In fact, I know so little about Mum's early life.'

Sarah's arm tightened around Deedee and with a smile, she continued, 'Then let me tell you.'

And so, Deedee learned more in the next half an hour about her mother's life than she had learned in all the years she had lived with Minnie and Alice. Perhaps this had been a well-meaning attempt by her aunts to shield her and permit the young Deedee to live her own life and not be held back by the trauma from events long gone. But as the recollections flowed, she found herself welcoming them and forming images in her mind of the young Sarah and her adventures with Maggie. As Sarah's voice wove stories about the two young women and their time at nursing college, Deedee found herself flicking over the pages of the photo album, without conscious thought, picking up photos that were lying loosely between the pages, and now staring intently at the people captured in that moment of time. Images of two young women laughing with arms around each other, often in the company of others. At the beach, out dining, dressed in formal attire, and one photo looking as though they must have been at some sort of official event. Both ladies in immaculate nursing uniforms, lined up with other similarly attired young women waiting to have their hand shaken by a scary, much older nurse.

Deedee learned how her parents first met—her dad was a patient at the hospital who somehow managed to get hold of Maggie's contact details and pursue her relentlessly. A short courtship and a happy marriage.

'By the time you were born, I was already a mother of two—Harry and Lachlan—so I was able to offer support to Maggie and pass on baby clothes and toys, that sort of thing. Even though we didn't see each other that often, we kept in touch. We talked on the phone when we could, and we wrote to each other. People still wrote letters in those days. And then we would see each other when she came to stay with Minnie and Alice. I don't need to tell you how distraught we all were when your parents died. A terrible time, but the only consolation was that you survived, by pure chance. Sometimes I think your existence, and the need to give you a loving upbringing, was all that kept Alice and Minnie going in the years that followed. Sad times, but they did everything they could to protect you.'

Deedee nodded thoughtfully as she once more examined the photo she was still holding. There might be a black hole inside her where her parents were concerned, but the love and care she had received from Minnie and Alice had never been in any doubt. But was it enough? Even now as an adult woman nearing thirty years of age, she still was not so sure it was.

*

Deedee was silent on the drive back to Yass, her mind mulling over all of Sarah's stories. Stories of two young women and their adventures, their loves, and their excitement in creating futures for themselves, unaware one of them would have her future abruptly cut short. From time to time, she would glance down at the photo of the young Deedee in the arms of her laughing father, being fussed over by a mother who clearly cared about her daughter, or at the very least cared about protecting her from sunburn. *If she could see my weathered face now, I would probably be in trouble,* she thought.

'Penny for them,' asked Harry, as he briefly glanced across at her before resuming his forward examination of the road.

'Not worth that much,' she replied. 'Just contemplating all that your mother told me about my mum. Building up a picture of my mother. You know, Alice and Minnie never talked about her much—maybe to spare themselves—and me too I suppose. Occasionally, I would be told how my mannerisms were just like Mum's, but never did they talk about what she liked or about her early days as a young woman—what she got up to, how she met dad, all that sort of stuff. It's a bit overwhelming but somehow, I think once I have time to process all I have learned today, I suspect I will be back for more. It's like I now need to know.'

'Well, Mum will be up for it—anytime. There's nothing she likes more than a good natter. And she likes you. I could see that. Sorry you didn't get to meet my father or brother. Next time perhaps. There will be a next time, won't there?' An anxious tone had crept into Harry's voice.

'Of course. Mind you, I might be bringing Minnie with me. She was making noises about visiting the farm at some stage. Will it be okay if I bring her with me next time I visit? She can keep me company while I sketch.'

'Or she can keep Mum company. I suspect that is what will happen. So long as she doesn't let slip the purpose of any visit. I want your painting to remain a surprise. We'll have to think up a good excuse for another visit.'

'She won't say a word so long as I explain the need for secrecy. Look how she has kept silent all these years about Mum and Dad.' As she said this, Deedee was conscious of some feelings of resentment. *Surely her great-aunt should have understood how much a little girl needed to know about where she had come from. If that had occurred, maybe she wouldn't have felt so lost and alone throughout her childhood—the only companions she could rely on being a black cat and a small ghost child. How pathetic.*

As if reading her thoughts, Harry spoke. 'Don't be too hard on them. Those great aunts of yours did their best. Like you, they might have been out of their depth. It's not like in those days there was a manual on how to deal with grief and trauma. It might be different now with all those therapists hanging around, but back then people just got on with it and tried to manage. While things were not said overtly, I suspect the entire community rallied behind the aunts and did their best to support them and you. Like we have always done whenever disaster hits.'

Deedee, feeling drained of all emotion, said nothing. When they reached the gate at Minnie's house, she remembered her manners enough to thank Harry for the outing, and to assure him there was no need for him to come in.

'I'll be fine. Minnie will be inside somewhere, and I'll need to see if she needs any jobs doing. Thank you again. The day has been much more than I expected. Your farm is amazing, and I will be honoured to try and paint it for you. I've got a few photos on my phone, I'll use those to play with some sketches to work out what would be the best angle for a painting, and then you can inspect. I suppose you'll be here sometime soon?' she asked, trying not to sound eager. Distressing day or not, she still wanted to see this man again.

'Sure thing. I'll get cracking on the verandah next week, in between my other jobs. Not sure which day I'll be here yet.'

Although Deedee felt like her world had changed so much in a few hours, nothing seemed to have changed here. The flaking white gate still scraped on the ground as she forced it open. The garden assumed a watchful hush as she walked along the brick lined stone path, almost as if it were holding its breath to see what would happen next, and Merlin was sitting outside the side door, in a patch of sunlight, continuing with his perpetual grooming. He paused at her approach and contemplated this human. Grooming forsaken, he stretched and approached Deedee for a pat, as was his due. A cursory sniff of her jeans confirming her contact with another animal, he turned and walked to the side door as if by silent order commanding her, his servant, to open it.

Inside, there was no sign of Minnie. Deedee walked to the kitchen—not there. To the spare bedroom—not there. And then, with a call up the stairs, she could hear a faint reply.

'Up here. In the bedroom.'

The voice she heard was so faint and quavery that Deedee immediately panicked and ran up the steep stairs, black cat scampering in front of her.

The door to the bedroom was open, but largely blocked by several bulging plastic garbage bags. Pushing some aside, she squeezed through the doorway and found her great-aunt seated on the bed that she had once shared with Alice. She was perched on the edge, holding a scrunched multi-coloured shawl tightly to her chest, looking lost in thought.

'Aunt. Are you ok?'

Minnie looked up with an unfocussed gaze and, as if dragging her thoughts from a place and time so far away, registered who was standing there. It took a few moments as her gaze sharpened and then with obvious affection she spoke.

'Don't mind me Deedee. I was a million miles away. Old memories. I thought it was time to sort out Alice's stuff, but somehow it all got a bit too much. I made a start. You can't have missed all those garbage bags blocking the way. It wasn't too hard when I was just sorting through jeans, jumpers and stuff, but then I got to the special items—you know, like this,' she said holding up the shawl for Deedee to inspect. 'We bought this when we were in Italy years ago, on one of those 'spur of the moment' holidays. I saw it in a shop window and knew it was a perfect present for Alice. I snuck out of our hotel when she was having a nap, and raced back to the shop which, fortunately was open. I haggled like I was born to do it, and surprised Alice with this shawl that night when we were dressing for dinner.'

Minnie smiled, the memory clearly a happy one. With a chuckle she continued, 'I can still see her in my mind's eye, fussing over what to wear, dressed in one of those floaty dresses she so loved. You remember those hippie chick numbers? And going on about how it would be cold later and she had nothing warm. I produced this shawl, wrapped it around her and we had a wonderful night out, sitting outside until the wee small hours, eating too much. We definitely drank way too much and just enjoyed being there with each other.' Minnie considered the shawl again. 'No, this one cannot be thrown away. I think it now belongs to you,' she said as she wrapped the shawl around a teary Deedee. 'It seems like it is my lot to keep on gifting this shawl. I hope it brings you much joy and brings back many happy memories.' Minnie gazed affectionately at her great-niece. Her gaze sharpened, and with an unexpected burst of energy, she lurched off the bed and headed for the door.

'Enough of this. There's only so much tidying up a person can do. I can hear the gin and tonics calling from here—fancy joining me? After all, don't you need to tell me what you have been up to all day.'

Chapter Twenty

Deedee's dramatic dream swirled around her in episodic chaos. One moment she was running around the garden chasing, and being chased by, Bertie. The next she was down by the river being restrained by a shadowy person she just KNEW had to be Julian. Trapped, wanting to escape, yet somehow also wanting to surrender. Then, the shadow morphed into Harry who, with gentle arms, pulled her closer and leaned forward as if to kiss her. Harry? No way! Even in her dream state she felt a moment of surprise. Harry and her? Surely that scruffy person was not the one her subconscious fancied. She felt herself slide deeper and closer to the 'dream' Harry as the background noise increased. An insistent ringing that would not go away. How could she focus on all this drama when a cacophony kept intruding?

Then, with dawning awareness, she realised the noise was in fact her phone ringing from where she had placed it on the bedside table. Staring blearily at the display, she could see the caller was her Sydney housemate. Deedee reluctantly answered as. she had a feeling she knew why he would be calling. It was about time she made a decision about her future. Should she stay with Minnie or should she return to Sydney?

After a short but friendly discussion, Deedee ended the call and lay back in her bed staring thoughtfully at the ceiling. Not noticing the water stains from the long history of a leaking roof, nor the flaking paint, she mulled over the topic of her phone conversation.

It was just as she had suspected—her flatmate was anxious to find out what her plans were.

'Of course I miss having you around Deedee, but I was wondering … if you don't intend to return, would you mind if I took over the lease and maybe bought some of the furniture from you? I suppose this is not something you have really been thinking about, but it would suit me as I am hoping my girlfriend will move in with me. It's been a few weeks since you left and although this might be a bit premature, I thought I should make contact to find out what your plans might be.'

Just like that the universe realigned and Deedee's future became clear. Her obligations to her home in Sydney could now easily be disentangled, leaving her free to return to *this* home— and to Minnie. Lying on the bed, now becoming aware of the flaking ceiling, Deedee wondered how she felt about her future not only being manipulated by fate in this manner, but how it lacked the need for conscious thought by her. Yet, for some inexplicable reason, she didn't mind. The thought of staying in this small town with her great-aunt somehow felt as if that is how it should be—as if she had reached a point in her life where returning home was not a burden, but more a relief. There was no longer anything to run away from. Maybe it was a maturity thing but having spent some time away, she now had a standard against which to measure the prospect of living in a small town. This small community no longer felt as confining as it did when she was in her teens. Something inside her had shifted. Unlike other times, she now realised that the recent close proximity to Minnie, while still occasionally causing tension, had mostly been a surprisingly easy adjustment. Perhaps the change in her views had been brought about by the growing realisation of how little time was left for the two of them to be together. She knew that she would regret it for the rest of her life if she ran back to Sydney and neglected her great-aunt. Maybe one day when Minnie was no longer alive, she could think of returning to a life by the sea. Yet, as she lay back and listened to the bird call in the garden, she thought there were still reasons aplenty to enjoy living here. The garden, the birdlife, the company of that Bertie, and of course, the studio. A rush of energy caused her to sit upright.

The studio! Of course! Why lie in bed when the studio was calling? So much to do. The paintings she had been working on as a present for Minnie had mentally been discarded as she thought of the challenge of painting that scene for Harry. She had the photos and a few quick sketches she could use as a guide, but she really needed to get started. The question of determining how to capture that scene intrigued her. Watercolour, acrylic or gouache? What would be appropriate? She would need to experiment before she could even begin to think of starting the final work. Usually, Deedee knew exactly how she would paint the illustrations that were her day-to-day business—a simple sketch infilled with watercolour. But this task was totally different, and for that reason it filled her with excitement. A project that would stretch her skills and be different to anything she had done before was exactly what she needed. And it had to be good so it would make a suitable companion to hang next to Alice's artwork.

Deedee jumped out of bed and scurried around trying to find suitable clothes to wear. Old jeans that had been discarded on the floor would be just fine for today's work. She pulled on a grotty T-shirt, a rather stained sweatshirt, and a pair of boots that had been shoved under the bed. Scraping her hair back with some bobby pins, Deedee realised that at this moment she didn't exactly look attractive—but she didn't care. Her attire was perfectly suitable for a day being spent as an artist.

Heading down the stairs, her mind was already focussed on the work she had planned for the day. But thoughts of Minnie intruded. She couldn't sneak out without letting her aunt know her plans for the day. A cup of tea in bed for Minnie that would give her the opportunity to tell her where she would be all day and let her check that her aunt was doing ok. After all that emotion yesterday, it was possible that Minnie was not managing so well. She needed to check in on her—just in case.

*

'Minnie, are you awake?'

A soft voice intruded Minnie's dreams of times long ago—a voice she somehow knew but couldn't place. The voice spoke again, and Minnie knew she must respond.

'Alice?' she quavered.

'No, dear. It's not Alice. It's just me—Deedee. I've brought you a cup of tea. But stay in bed. It's still early. Here. I'll leave it on your bedside table. I'm heading up to the studio, and chances are I will be up there all morning. I want to get started on a new painting It's still rather cold this morning, so I wouldn't rush out of bed if I were you.'

Minnie rolled over. Hearing the chinking sound of the china being deposited on the small wooden bedside table and feeling a soft kiss on her forehead, she permitted herself to give a small grunt in acknowledgement before settling back into her dream. Now, where was she? Oh yes, in times long ago—when she was young, attractive and full of energy. When she felt like she could do anything, *be* anything, and life's adventures spread out before her in a limitless array.

She was a young woman when she first arrived in this small country town to take up an administrative job at the local council. A woman of about 28, much the same age as Deedee was now. Her studies at university were complete and her first job long behind her. This new job was an opportunity to extend her skills and to create a new life for herself away from the pain of a recently broken heart. From the very first days, she knew she had come home. The people in this small town welcomed her and involved her in its dramas. Being at the local council, it was easy for Minnie to get to know many of the community as so much of her working life brought them into contact with her. It was through meeting the locals that she became aware of how Harry's grandfather was planning to sell his cottage home. One look and she was smitten—with the cottage that is, not with Harry's grandfather. Negotiations were straightforward. In fact, Minnie suspected that the selling price was a secondary consideration to the need to be assured that the new owner would care for this much-loved family home. Strangely enough, there was no mention of the resident ghosts during the sale negotiations. Perhaps it wasn't necessary as not everyone saw, nor felt, the other members of the household. It took a while for Minnie to become aware that she shared the house and garden with others. Being a pragmatic person, she accepted their presence and simply got on with her own life. The boy child in the garden—Bertie—was no trouble at all. At times she even enjoyed his company. Although occasionally she was inclined to resent his random moving of her gardening tools, which would necessitate a rather sharp rebuke from her. She learned fairly quickly that the spirit ladies in the parlour could be trying with their particular ways, but at least they remained confined to that room. So long as she kept a respectful distance, and didn't move the parlour furniture, they kept quiet, only occasionally making their presence known by dimming the lights, moving or hiding the ornaments. Not that Minnie minded if the ornaments were hidden. So many items in that room came with the house and were really not to her taste. She often suspected they belonged to the old ladies and were tied to the house—just like those two.

She hadn't been in the house all that long when she met Alice. Their first meeting was no longer that clear in her muddled recollections, but then again not much else was. Minnie may have been confused about the actual occasion, but the initial impression— that sense of connection—still lingered in her jumbled memories. That and the way their relationship flourished from a friendship to close friendship, to so much more. It seemed like only a moment from when they first met that Alice moved herself, her paints, and her flamboyant attire into the cottage, and into Minnie's life. Looking back on it, Minnie was still amazed at how accepting the small community was of the same sex relationship her and Alice shared. It was still a small conservative town in those days, yet somehow most people in the town were accepting of the love these two women shared. It may have had something to do with Alice being an artist. Creative people and their unusual lifestyles seemed to be tolerated— being different from others was almost expected from an artist. Of course, there were a few people, largely from the more established families, that if they acknowledged Minnie and Alice at all, they did it in such a cool manner that it was clear no further contact would be encouraged. Not that Minnie and Alice minded this treatment for they had very little in common with such people. In any event, they were so happy in their own little bubble that little else intruded.

The shocking death of Deedee's parents, and her arrival into the community, did much to attract the sympathy of so many of their neighbours. It probably helped that the young Deedee, with her wild curls and large chocolatey eyes, was such a beauty. It was hard not to like her. This, and her obvious trauma, ensured such ongoing support from the community—apart from the bullies—they could never be assuaged whatever the situation.

Minnie, lost in the memories of those times long ago, slumbered on—cup of tea forgotten and long gone cold. When she finally woke, she furtively, and with great care, poured the beverage out the bedroom window and into the garden. There was no need to tell Deedee she hadn't drunk it.

*

It was late in the afternoon when Deedee finally emerged from the studio. Overall, she was happy with her progress on what she now was referring to as 'Harry's commission'. The type of paint she would use for the painting was still unresolved. Much would depend upon the size of the painting, and to sort that out she would need to speak to Harry. With a few preliminary ideas now drying on the easels, that was enough for today. Hunger was driving her towards the house. With luck, her great-aunt might have prepared something for lunch, and there might even be some leftovers. But knowing her aunt's erratic cooking skills, she was not so sure that would be the case.

Down at the house she found her aunt ensconced in the sunroom chatting with Harry who, in between mouthfuls of what

Deedee took to be the leftover lunch, was doing his best to respond to the grilling from Minnie.

'Yes, of course Minnie,' he mumbled through a rather full mouth. 'I'll take those bags to the charity shop. If there's any more just let me know and I'll come and collect them from you.'

At Deedee's arrival, they both looked up with equally welcoming smiles on their faces.

'There you are dear. Just in time for a hot drink. Nothing left to eat I'm afraid. Harry took it all,' Minnie said as if it was all Harry's fault.

'Sorry. I didn't know you had yet to eat,' Harry blushed in response, passing his plate across. 'Here, take the last of this pie. It's rather good you know. Where have you been?'

'I've started on your painting and now need some input from you. Maybe after we finish this and before you head off, I could have a few minutes of your time?'

'Sure,' he said standing and wiping his hands on already greasy overalls. 'Okay with you Minnie if I grab that cuppa later?'

He was clearly keen to see what Deedee had been doing. As Harry headed for the door, Deedee scoffed the leftovers, shrugged at her aunt, and followed him.

Harry's enthusiasm for the test paintings was gratifying, but not helpful.

'I like them all. You say you're not sure what paint to use. Can't help you with that I'm afraid. Whatever you think looks best. You mean it affects the end size of the picture? Why? Oh, now I understand. You can get a bigger canvas if you use acrylics, but if you use watercolour paints, you're restricted to a smaller size of watercolour paper. Well, I never! I suppose this stuff is not really something I ever think about. But you're the expert. You choose. Why can't you do the same size picture as Alice? Oh, I get it, you're not doing oil paints. But you could do similar size if you painted on a canvas. Not with paper though? It's doing my head in Deedee, you work it out. I'm just a simple gardener and whatever you do will be fine with me,' he smiled. 'You're the expert and I trust you to get it right—really.' The trust shone right at her out of those brown/green eyes.

'Alright. I'll give it a bit more thought. I could stick with using watercolour and I think it would look pretty good—and that is what I know I am good at. But I do wonder if I should be brave and try a different sort of approach.'

'My suggestion? Be brave. Go for something new. If it doesn't work, then there is always the fallback position of doing the safe approach. But who knows? You might surprise yourself.'

They both turned to examine the practice paintings displayed before them, the identical scene interpreted in different media. The same yet different.

'You know each painting has a different mood. The watercolour lends itself to a softer, more atmospheric mood and the other two are more dramatic. What do you want to achieve?' Harry asked as he moved along considering each painting in turn.

'I don't know. I'll have to think on it. You're right though. It's more than just what sort of paint to use and how to get the image just right. It is also what sort of mood I want to convey. And maybe Alice's painting is relevant to that. Do I want something that is a complete contrast to her painting to show how different the setting can be? Maybe I do. But I suspect that is enough thinking for today. I think I'll sleep on it.'

'Great! You can help me then.'

'Help you? Haven't I done enough in the garden?'

'Not the garden! Keep up! I need you to help me measure the verandah so I can work out what timber to buy. I'll start on that tomorrow.'

Their progress down the curved garden path towards the front of the cottage was slow. Firstly, because they were ambushed by Scruff, who made his enthusiasm at finding them both safe and unscathed known by bouncing up and down on them both, and then by Harry's need to pause every few steps to inspect a blossom, pull out a weed, or investigate some other insignificant matter. In the end, Deedee grabbed Harry by the arm and dragged him along.

'Come on. We haven't got all day. You've got bags to move after you've done this measuring, and I have dinner to prepare. Are you always so easily distracted?'

'Yep. Now here's another distraction. Remember I mentioned the spring ball? It's on this weekend. Fancy coming with me?'

He turned towards her in anticipation—eyes hopeful, expression open. Deedee, mindful of her recent dream involving Harry in an amorous embrace, puzzled the significance of this invitation. What did he intend? Was this a date or just an opportunity for an outing? In the seconds that passed, as she considered her response, Harry's expression changed from open to anxious and before she could speak, he continued.

'Sorry. Maybe it's a bad idea. I just thought that seeing you seem to be staying here, it might help to get to know a few more of the locals,' he said. 'And it is a bit of fun. But if you don't want to do it, forget I asked.' As he turned to move further along the path, Deedee put out her hand and touched his arm. He stopped and turned to look at her, hope flaring in his eyes once more.

'No, it's fine. I just wasn't expecting you to ask me to a ball. I've never been to one before. Is it fancy? I think I would like to come so long as it isn't too formal. I can't dance you see.'

'It might be called a ball, but really it's pretty basic. It's held in the community hall. We have a band and a bit of dancing, and a supper in the adjoining supper room. Nothing to worry about. Just a bit of fun and a chance for everyone to forget the everyday. And to get dressed up of course. There's a theme, something to do with spring, but not everyone bothers about that. If you want to join me, I'll pick you up about 7:00 on Saturday night—this Saturday night coming. I'll double-check on the theme and let you know in case you want to find a costume.' As if an afterthought, he added, 'And don't worry about not being able to dance—neither can I!' With a smile he handed her a tape measure, and they started the process of measuring up the verandah.

Clearly, as far as Harry was concerned, the conversation was over, but Deedee continued to mull over this invitation in between writing down measurements. A ball—and a spring ball at that. Should she go? Although it did appear that Harry had assumed she would be going with him. What was causing her to hold back? It was just an invitation to an outing, not a romantic date. She would be sharing the evening with a roomful of people. Why then was she not so effusive in her response? Was she scared?

Later on, while sitting by the fire with Minnie sipping a pre-dinner gin and tonic, she mentioned it. She was still puzzled about why she felt so ambivalent about the whole matter.

'Harry has invited me to the spring ball this weekend. I'm not sure whether I should go.'

'Why not? They're a lot of fun. Alice and I used to go every year when we were so much younger and had the energy. It is always a good night—for a range of reasons. Some of the outfits—Oh My God! They would reek of mothballs, especially the gentlemen's evening suits. And the dancing! Some of it was so creative. It gave us plenty to laugh about. You must go my dear. It's not good for you spending every evening with little old me. A bit of fun would do you no harm. Now what's the theme? I'm sure we can find an outfit for you somewhere.'

Chapter Twenty-One

It was the night of the spring ball— a fine, clear night—cool but not quite balmy. It was early spring after all and the tail end of winter was still making its presence felt. Minnie fussed over her great-niece as she was waiting for Harry to arrive.

'Make sure you take a shawl; you may need it. Not only outside, but possibly also inside the hall. The heating there is pretty much non-existent. It's really only body warmth that will warm things up, or a bit of dancing,' she smiled, as if recalling happy memories. 'Stop fidgeting my dear and let me look at you.' Still holding onto Deedee but with arms outstretched, she stepped back and with head tilted to one side, she considered her great-niece.

'So lovely you are. Like a goddess of spring. Aren't I clever to have found something of Alice's that I hadn't yet thrown out? It's perfect, don't you think? My darling Alice would have loved to see you in this dress.'

Deedee thoughtfully considered her image in the full-length mirror. Quite a change from her usual style. She was dressed in one of Alice's full-length, flowing silk numbers of various colours—multiple shades of green, complemented by hints of peach and pink, in a swirling design. It had long, loose hanging sleeves—almost medieval in their shape—the fabric so sheer that it rippled and swirled as she moved. Her hair was styled into curls that clustered tightly around her dainty head, a shimmering golden cord wound through them. Dangly earrings that sparkled with every movement, completed the look.

A knock at the side door made them turn and move away. Minnie rushed to open the door and greeted Harry with enthusiasm.

'Well, I never! Look at you in your formal gear. You and Deedee are going to be totally unrecognisable at the ball. Totally transformed you both are. Come in and meet your partner. I feel I should introduce you, as she is not the Deedee you are used to.'

Harry smiled in embarrassment. He fidgeted at his collar with one hand as if trying to loosen the bow tie that had been hand tied around his neck. A man not used to wearing a tie it would appear. The formal dinner suit clung to his tall frame and showed his broad shoulders and long legs to best effect. There was no odour of moth balls emanating from this suit. It was, as he later explained, a purchase made not that long ago for the purpose of accompanying his sister to some fancy 'do' in Canberra. His reaction upon catching sight of Deedee was almost comical—a gape-mouthed stare of amazement and, after a pause, he praised her.

'Jeez, I wouldn't have recognised you in that fancy gear! So floaty. You're almost girly in that dress.'

'I'll take that as a compliment,' Deedee smiled as she swirled around to better display her outfit. And then, taking a shawl and a vintage, black beaded evening bag where they had been left on the side table, she headed for the door, giving Minnie a quick peck on the cheek on her way out.

'Don't wait up for me Aunt. I could be late. I have a key and can let myself in.'

'Of course, dear. I'll leave the porch light on. Have fun the two of you.'

'We will,' they both chorused and headed off into the night.

The hall was just a short distance away. It was located on the main street and although it was possible to walk there, Deedee was grateful they drove. The unaccustomed high heels were already making their presence felt, and she tried not to think about how her feet would feel by the end of the evening.

Fortunately, their arrival at the hall provided her with sufficient distraction from her complaining feet. The exterior of the hall was a mass of sparkling lights which disguised the prosaic nature of the weatherboard structure. A mass of people already clustered around the entrance greeted their approach with whistles and cheers—largely directed at Harry. Unaccustomed to this kind of attention from strangers, Deedee was not sure how to respond. She clutched her shawl tightly around herself and glanced at Harry. Unlike her, he was basking in all the attention, waving royally to his audience, and grinning. He took Deedee's hand and pulled it through his crooked arm.

'Come on princess, looks like we have made their day, or should I say evening. Let's get inside away from this lot. Maybe there's a better class of party goers inside.' He pushed his way through the groups of people exchanging greetings. Inside it was just as Minnie had predicted—vaguely warm from the huddles of people standing around the walls, or dancing in the middle of the hall. Deedee, having never been in this hall before, took a moment to pause and consider the sight arrayed before her. It was a simple construction. Not a grand city hall, but something with no pretensions of grandeur. The walls were lined with cream painted tongue and groove boards, the ceiling with pressed metal in a geometric pattern, and the stage at the far end of the room was of simple utilitarian construction that housed a four-piece rock'n'roll band fronted by an enthusiastic singer. All around her she could hear people chatting and laughing. In the middle of the floor a group of dancers was moving to the beat—some of them with more style than others. To her right there was an opening that, judging by the constant procession of people returning with full glasses of wine, beer and unidentifiable beverages, she assumed led to the bar.

Harry, seeing a group of his friends, led Deedee across. Some of them looked vaguely familiar to her and once introductions were made, she realised some were indeed old school mates. In a typical manner of small towns everywhere, everyone in the group greeted her warmly and immediately drew her into the conversation. Her aunt was known to all so the first few minutes were occupied with assuring them that her aunt had very much recovered. Amid such genuine concern, Deedee found it easy to relax into the conversation and enjoy the company of these new-found friends. That was until Harry interrupted.

'Come on. Enough chatting. It's time to dance.' With an imperious hand, he commanded her arm and manoeuvred Deedee onto the dance floor before she found time to object. Her muttered protests were brushed away like so many annoying flies.

'Just follow me. You'll be fine. Who knows, you might have fun.'

It only took a few moves for Deedee to realise that Harry not only looked good, but he also knew how to move. A man of hidden talents. In time with a rock'n'roll tune, he took command and led Deedee around the floor in a series of turns that she was powerless to resist. Now she understood why it was said that it was necessary for one dancer to lead and the other to follow. She did not need to know what to do as Harry, with each move and with varying pressure on her arm, made it clear what she had to do. With a firm grip, he pulled her close then pushed her away into a twirl. All she had to do was keep her balance and move as commanded in time to the music. By the time the tune had finished, they were both flushed and out of breath.

'That was amazing Harry. I meant it when I said I really can't dance, but somehow you made it happen. Can we do that again?'

And they did. Over and over again until, with sweat dripping from his brow and face flushed with exertion, Harry called a halt to the proceedings.

'Give a man a break. I need a beer. You are obviously so much fitter than me, but even you must need a drink and a rest.'

'Only if you promise that we can dance later again.'

'Deal.'

Arm in arm they headed across the dance floor, following other people headed for the bar. The rest of the evening passed in much the same way—dancing, drinking, maybe a bit of eating, and then further dancing. It was during a slow number, when they were dancing closely together, Deedee kept reminding herself—slow, slow, quick, quick. She felt a light tap on her shoulder and heard a familiar voice.

'Mind if I butt in Harry? Seems like you've been monopolising Deedee all night.'

Deedee stiffened but before she could react, Harry had released her and moved away, stating as he went. 'No worries, but I'll be back. Just one dance, understand?'

Another set of arms took hold of her and drew her close. Her stiffening spine obvious to the other person.

'Hey, relax. It's just a dance. Sorry I gave you a shock, but I figured you'd ignore me if I tried some other move.'

'Can you blame me for that?' she hissed at the person she had last seen in the café some days ago.

'I'm sorry. I was insensitive and spoke out of turn. Can you blame me? I was so excited about what we planned to do with that subdivision that I forgot you might feel otherwise. It was crass of me to speak that way. I don't know if you can forgive me, but can we start again?'

She looked up at this man who, only a few days ago, she had thought irresistible. He looked down at her face with a guileless and open expression. Could she trust him? Was that necessary? After all, they were only having a dance and not agreeing to anything further—certainly not a long-term relationship. But the firm clasp of his hands around hers, and the fresh smell of him, made her want to lean in further. Without conscious thought she leaned in, hip to hip, her chest pressing into his torso—not quite chest to chest as she was so much shorter than him. Despite herself, she had to admit he felt good—so good.

'Alright. Let's make a new start. Let's pretend we have never met. Now, I can't dance. Can you?'

'Just watch me and weep!'

Clasping her even tighter than Deedee thought possible, she felt herself being swirled around in a slow waltz—or at least she *thought* that was what it was. All she knew was that she could feel Julian's leg somehow pressing against hers and moving her around.

Meanwhile, his hand was pressed firmly on her back pushing her into him and around the dance floor. She felt herself awash with sensation. Her pulse was racing—not from the exertion, but from the excitement of being pressed so close to him. She longed to be pressed even closer, so that there was nothing between them.

The dance ended all too soon. It seemed to Deedee that Julian was reluctant to release her and as he stared down into her eyes, he smiled.

'Okay? Fancy another dance?'

With a shake of her head, she looked around for Harry. This Julian was way too dangerous, instinct told her that, but somehow …

She was relieved to see Harry approaching but soon registered the anxious look on his face.

'Harry, are you okay?'

'Not really. Mum just rang. Dad has had a fall and I have to get home to get him to hospital. Do you mind if I drop you off home now? I'm sorry to cut your evening short but I need to go.'

Deedee put her arm on Harry's, but before she could speak Julian cut in.

'Don't worry mate. I'll get her home safe and sound. You get going. Sounds like you haven't a moment to lose.'

'Are you okay with that Deedee?' It was clear by his frowning expression that Harry recalled her last encounter with Julian.

'No, it's fine. You go and look after things at home. I'll be fine,' said Deedee as she dismissed his words with a careless gesture. She was an adult and could manage perfectly well on her own. This over-protective approach was not something she was used to.

Harry waved and, squeezing his way through the crowd, he left the hall. Deedee watched him go, concern etched on her face.

'I hope his father is okay. I have only met his mother, but I got the impression that his family is close …' Deedee's voice petered out as she felt unable to articulate the general feeling of unease that was washing over her.

'Yeah, they're a close lot the Frost family. But come on. There's nothing we can do and worrying won't help. Anyway, why spoil the party? Another dance?'

Deedee nodded at Julian and, accepting his proffered hand, allowed herself to be led back onto the dance floor where it seemed like most of the party goers had gathered to celebrate with movement.

As they settled into a complementary rhythm, this time moving to a rock'n'roll song from the sixties, Deedee allowed herself a moment to examine her partner.

'You look different somehow. I get it that you would look different in formal gear rather than your jogging outfit, but there's something more.'

Julian smiled and with one hand, reached up to stroke his chin. Understanding dawning upon Deedee, she said, 'I get it! You've shaved! And you've combed your hair! You look so different. Almost stylish.'

'Almost?'

Well, actually more than stylish. But she wasn't going to tell him that. In his formal dinner suit that donned a plain black bow tie, he looked like a suave James Bond—a strong jaw and square chin now clearly revealed since the disguising beard had been removed. With his slicked back dark hair and gleaming dark eyes, he exuded animal magnetism like some untamed creature—a panther perhaps?

Pushing thoughts of their last toxic encounter aside, Deedee accepted that there was nothing to it but to enjoy his company and the evening. Not that this was a hardship. It appeared that Julian was also determined to make amends as he set out to entertain and charm his companion. They danced, laughed, drank, and ate until midnight had long passed. The dwindling crowds made it clear that the evening was almost over. Deedee's feet were now in open rebellion. Hobbling to a chair by the side wall, she sat down and removed her sandals.'

'That's better,' she sighed. 'I'm not putting them back on again,' she said as she rubbed her aching feet.

Julian, now sitting next to her, leaned in. 'Here let me. A foot massage is what you need and then maybe I should carry you to the car. Your feet have done enough work tonight.'

He carefully started massaging one foot, then the other. If Deedee could have purred, she would have. Such bliss. Tremors of pleasure vibrated through her as he rubbed the ball of each foot, stroked the arch, and gently pulled at each toe.

'Oh my, where did you learn such a technique? Give up your day job and I reckon you could earn a fortune with this talent.'

Julian smiled and said nothing. He just kept on with his rubbing and pressing until Deedee felt herself swept into another reality. She did not resist when he gently released her feet and, standing up, reached for her discarded shoes before sweeping her up into his arms in one swift movement.

'Let's give those feet a rest. My car is just outside. Time to go princess. Let me carry you there.'

As if she could resist. The cold air outside hit her like a ton of bricks, and she felt herself being jolted to awareness.

'Here. Let me down Julian, I can walk.' She squirmed in his arms, but they tightened as she spoke.

'No. Relax. The ground is wet. You won't like it. And anyway, here's the car.

The car—some sort of low-slung sporty thing—was comfortable and, once he had the heater going, felt rather warm. It didn't take long for Julian to drive to Deedee's home. Once there, they sat in silence. Deedee, uncertain as to what the protocol was for saying goodbye to a once loathed person with whom she now seemed to be on speaking terms, reached for her seat belt and slowly undid it. She reached forward to locate her shoes and bag in the foot well. Julian reached across and touched her on the arm, and she turned to look into those brooding eyes. She later realised that turning like that was her undoing. In hindsight, it was a mistake to linger in the car—or was it?

Things happened quickly after that. The burbling engine turned off and silence descended. Not that Deedee was aware of any silence. The noise of her heartbeat and pulse thrumming in her ears seemed to block out anything else. The tension she felt as he leaned in closer and closer to her was almost overwhelming. More than anything, at that moment she desired his touch. Perhaps the foot massage had been a precursor to what followed for she felt warm and open to whatever followed. His touch, his kiss and his exploration with questing hands were to an extent constrained by the confines of his European car. But as she soon discovered, with a flick of a switch, her car seat was soon laid flat, and their interactions continued. Her dress was pushed to one side as parts of Deedee were revealed to further exploration. It wasn't that Deedee wasn't doing any exploration of her own—Julian's shirt was unbuttoned and opened to reveal a broad chest. Thoughtfully, she leaned towards him and kissed those strong lips and determined chin before trailing her kisses further down. But her progress was impeded by a hand taking her by the chin and moving her face to his. They continued this way for what seemed like ages. With each kiss, caress and rub, Deedee's frustration built until, with one almighty shudder, she responded to the hand that had been stroking her between her legs. And then reality dawned. And embarrassment. What had she been thinking? Well, that was actually quite obvious. Pulling up her knickers and pulling down her dress, she sat up and opened the door.

'I have to go. Thanks for driving me home. And … and …' She didn't know what else to say. What was the protocol for farewells after an impromptu car romp?

Julian leaned towards her and looked up. "I suppose you need to go, but I really wish you wouldn't. Can I see you tomorrow?'

'Maybe.'

The gate gave its usual protesting squeak as she forced it open. Thankfully, with her entry to the garden, the motion sensor light came. She crept along the path anxious not to make a noise—a silent intruder not wanting to disturb the other residents of the garden. There was a floral scent of spring blossoms in the air as she made her way to the side door. Finding the key in her handbag, she quietly unlocked, and opened, the door. The last thing she needed at this moment was to be greeted by Minnie as she was sure that even the most basic cross-examination would result in her telling all.

The hall light, having been left on, cast a warm glow from its solitary bulb onto the reception committee. Not Minnie. Instead, a black cat that glared at her with golden eyes. If he could speak, she was sure Merlin was saying, *'Do you consider this a respectable time to get home? Explain yourself young lady.'*

Merlin stretched, and approached Deedee sniffing her bare feet and the hem of her dress. His reaction was immediate and obvious. With an arching of his back and a loud hiss, he glared at her once more before turning, tail in the air, and stalking off. There was no need for Merlin to speak any *human* language. With his every move, he made it clear he was unimpressed.

*

Warm and snug under her doona yet still awake, Minnie smiled when she heard the side door close. Her girl was back home. She hoped that the evening had been a success and maybe, just maybe, an evening spent together would further cement the bond between Harry and her beautiful girl. Little did she know how wrong she was!

Chapter Twenty-Two

When Deedee turned on her phone the next morning she was inundated with messages. Text messages from her housemate, her publisher, Julian, and Harry. She worked her way through them methodically. Her housemate's message was straightforward—a list of items of furniture he wanted to buy, with an offer to arrange the removalist to pack and deliver the rest to her. He was very logical and ordered, Deedee thought. Did he approach his life in such a systematic, yet boring way? Still, she was appreciative of him taking on this task, so she immediately responded, accepting his offer, and asking that the removalist quote be sent to her. Decision made and processes set—she felt an unexpected feeling of relief. Was that because the work associated with moving had been taken from her? Or was it because of other attractions in this small town?

The publisher's message was also direct and straight to the point. The final draft would be sent to her that day for her review, and it was hoped, her approval. Of course, she was advised there was the need for a quick turnover as 'deadlines were tight.' *Aren't they always*? she thought. Still, as soon as she received the document, she should be able to turn it around fairly quickly unless major changes had been made. Another straightforward message.

Then she turned to Harry's text. It was brief. An apology for having to rush off the previous evening, and an update on his father's condition. He had sprained his ankle. After waiting for what seemed like hours in the emergency department at the hospital, he was X-rayed, the sprain diagnosed, and he was sent home with a strapped ankle and painkillers. He said his dad was miserable, complaining about his enforced inactivity and would most likely suffer more from boredom and being kept cooped up indoors, than from the actual injury. There was nothing for Deedee to do there but respond with positive words and acknowledge that she appreciated being taken to the spring ball. There was no need to indicate how *much* she appreciated it!

Turning to Julian's text, she paused and considered her feelings before she started to read it. The previous night's experience had turned out to be totally unexpected, but when she thought about it, also unsurprising. She had felt that there was some element of unfinished business in her connection with Julian. When she walked away that morning after their dispute, there had been some feelings of regret that she would never get to explore the electricity between them, to find out whether there was something more between them. A potential relationship perhaps? Well now she had. Was what they had relationship material? Or was it just animal magnetism? Not that the latter was unattractive. Her life was such a desert that any contact was better than nothing.

Reading Julian's text, she smiled.

Good morning gorgeous. Hope you slept well, and have the feet recovered? How about lunch today? 12:30 at our usual café? Jules xxx

Kisses? What did that signify? She thought back to the feelings he had awoken in the night before and as she leaned back in her bed, she relived their interaction—the dancing, the close connection, and then the even closer connection in the car outside the front gate. This was more excitement than she had experienced in months. Of course, she would go to lunch with him. The thought of sitting near him, legs in contact, hands touching, and maybe something more later—how could she refuse?

Even as she typed her enthusiastic reply, a voice in her mind reminded her not to be too trusting—that Julian was not necessarily as perfect as she was wishing him to be. A reminder that she blithely ignored.

But not completely. Something held her back from mentioning this lunch date to her great-aunt. Not that Minnie was all that interested in her plans for the day. She was too focussed on the events of the previous evening—who was there, what were they wearing, and how had she enjoyed the night? The news of Harry's abrupt departure, and the reason why, evoked some consternation, which was assuaged to some extent when Deedee read out that morning's text message from Harry.

Deedee finished her toast, drank the last of her tea, pushed her chair back from the table and got up.

'I'm off to the studio today Minnie. Don't worry about lunch for me. I've got heaps to do. I'm working on that painting for Harry, and the publisher wants me to review the proof copy of that *Wendy Witch* story. I'll take some fruit up with me and maybe go for a walk if I need a break. I'll see you late this afternoon.'

Deedee felt bad about not being entirely truthful with her aunt. Of course, she was going to do all those things she had mentioned. It was just that something was making her hold back from mentioning Julian. Maybe that something related to how he had spoken about wanting to buy her aunt's home. Again, that niggling feeling, that sense that perhaps seeing more of Julian was not a great idea—a feeling that she resolutely pushed aside. She had agreed to lunch with the man, she hadn't made a lifetime commitment to him. What could possibly go wrong?

The morning passed quickly. Knowing how bossy the publisher could be, she focussed first on reviewing the final draft of the story that had been emailed to her. She was not surprised to find it all looked good—as she would expect it to be coming from *this* publisher and team. They were so well organised and methodical. Her illustrations had been accepted without objection by either the author or the publisher—even the image involving the magical creatures in the vegetation had been included. The colours in the images were vibrant and so close to her original paintings that she was rather impressed. Her only query, a minor one at that, involved the placement of words and an image on one of the pages. After sending a quick email off to the publisher, Deedee focussed on painting the farm scene.

It was just as well she had set an alarm. Being so heavily immersed as she was in the creation of the scene, she lost all track of time. When the alarm sounded, it felt like an irritant dragging her back from some other reality—a reality in which she had been completely absorbed in the sweep of colour. Her mind was solely and deeply focussed on the need to somehow capture the changing light of the landscape—the reflections on the river, the shadows under the gum trees, and the lengthening afternoon glow on the hills on the other side of the river. She was so absorbed in this landscape that it took some time for her to register the beep of the alarm, and when she did it was with some reluctance that she allowed herself to be dragged away from this other world and back to reality.

Then it dawned on her. She had a lunch date and here she was in jeans and a T-shirt. They were only slightly paint bespattered. But they weren't very dressy. Did that matter? After all, less than 24 hours ago this man had seen her almost naked, and anyway, it was only up at the local café—not some posh place. Grabbing her leather coat from the back of the chair, Deedee raced out the door. There was no way she could go back to the house and change, for that would result in a cross-examination by Minnie—definitely something to be avoided. Julian would just have to accept her as he found her.

'Been painting, have we?' asked Julian, wiping a paint splatter off her cheek. They had settled at a table in the rear courtyard of the local café—a lucky find as the place was bustling with the hungry lunchtime crowd. Having placed their orders with a very efficient waitress, they were now seated side by side. Conversation had been sporadic. Now that she was here, Deedee found herself at a loss as to what to say. She knew so little about this man—apart from what he felt like and how he smelled—and she couldn't talk to him about that, could she? She wracked her mind as to what to say. Running—he liked running—yes, that would do.

'Did you go running today?' she asked, hoping the subject would keep the conversation going for a little while.

'No, I slept in. I was too tired to go,' Julian said with a smirk. 'Maybe we could meet tomorrow and go for a jog.' With a wiggle of his eyebrows and a suggestive leer, his expression hinted that he had something more in mind.

'Maybe.' Somehow Deedee felt faintly miffed. She wasn't too sure she liked his suggestion. Like she was a pushover.

Their food arrived, and the conversation moved onto other topics—topics largely involving Julian—Deedee couldn't help noticing. He spoke at length about his fancy apartment and busy life in Sydney, and how he had come back for the spring ball but would soon be heading back. He gave the impression that his life was just one big social whirl. Was he trying to impress her? Deedee felt the need to explain how she was leaving Sydney behind and moving back to live with her aunt.

With a shrug, Julian acknowledged the bad timing of her move.

'Pity, we could have seen much more of each other in Sydney.' The all too familiar leer made its appearance again. Deedee suppressed a shudder. 'Still, I get back here fairly regularly to see the folks and help out where they need me to. We could still keep in contact—you know, Skype every night.' His expression made it obvious what he had in mind.

Barely able to repress her revulsion, Deedee moved the conversation onto safer topics. She copied his method of conversation and spoke about herself, her love of painting and her current projects.

'A landscape for Harry, you say? Now there's an idea. I could get you to do something for me. Of course, it would depend how much you charge. I am guessing you do 'mate's rates'? That's the only way Harry could afford it of course.'

Deedee's eyes flashed with indignation. What a put down to her *and* Harry!

'I definitely don't do what you call 'mate's rates'! I'm a professional and to be honest, I am fully booked for months to come. My services as an illustrator are highly sought after and I only agreed to squeeze in Harry's commission as a favour. He does so much for my aunt that I really felt I owed him.' Deedee fixed him with a steely gaze and continued, 'If you really want something, you will have to wait—at least six months. I can give you a cost estimate, but there will be no discount. I don't do discounts.'

He held his hands up in mock surrender and laughed. 'Okay, Okay, I get it. I'll wait. Some things are worth waiting for and it will give me an excuse to contact you.' This time his smile seemed genuine but so unsettling. One moment she dismissed him as a creep, then the next he looked like someone she would like to know more about—a gorgeous person at that. Even today, dressed in jeans, riding boots and a blue and white checked collared shirt, he was simply irresistible—the shadow of unshaven whiskers contouring the strong lines of his face, his dark eyes twinkling at her in amusement. It was obvious that he was no fool, and for a moment she suspected he was playing her like a fish. But why? What was his motive? Was it lust or was it something else? If only she could trust him.

Deedee looked down at her watch and shook her head. 'Look, I'm sorry but I have to go. I have much more to do in the studio this afternoon. I'll pay my half on the way out.'

'No way. My shout. I asked *you* out. See you tomorrow morning, same time?' He looked almost hopeful.

'Of course. And thank you for lunch.'

'It wasn't much. Soup and coffee. But I hope we can do it again.'

After saying goodbye, Deedee wandered thoughtfully down the main street, pondering their meeting. She couldn't get a bearing on this man. But having not really spent a lot of time with him, she didn't have much to go on. Sometimes it was hard to look past the physical beauty of the man and ignore the tug of attraction. But what was behind all that perfection? She was not so sure. He seemed to send out mixed messages and, she had to admit, a lot of those messages were about himself—how 'great' he was and what he wanted. An image of Harry sprung to mind. He was so straightforward—what you saw was what you got. There was no confusion in her mind when she thought of him, no subconscious warning that he might be dangerous, like the warning she sensed every time she got close to Julian. Somehow, she felt she could trust Harry, whereas she wasn't sure the same would apply to Julian. Maybe there was something wrong with her when it was this sense of danger that she found more attractive.

The afternoon dragged on. Try as she might, Deedee found she couldn't settle back to her work. The immersion in the task she had found so easily in the morning, had deserted her. Eventually, having to admit defeat, she cleaned and tidied away her paintbrushes, closed the studio door, and headed back down the path for the house.

The fire was lit inside the house but there was no sign of her aunt. Deedee wandered throughout the house, calling as she went. She wasn't in the kitchen, or in her bedroom. Deedee finally located her in the front parlour, sitting forlorn and silent, contemplating a letter held in shaking hands. Minnie was so lost in her thoughts she failed to register the presence of her great-niece until she sat on the lounge beside her. Reaching out with a comforting arm, she pulled her close.

'Minnie, what's wrong? I've been looking everywhere for you. Are you okay?'

Without saying a word, Minnie passed the letter across to her great-niece. Deedee read it slowly and silently and then looked up as the significance of the words registered.

'They can't do that, can they?'

'I don't know.' Tears streamed down Minnie's cheeks, finding their way down the furrowed wrinkles that mapped her face.

Deedee reconsidered the letter. Bearing an impressive logo, it appeared to be from the local council. Despite the turgid language in which it was framed, the meaning was clear. The council was giving notice of its intent to resume Minnie's property for the purpose of creating a road to provide safe access to a new residential subdivision that would be constructed in the area adjacent her land. There was a lot more detail in the letter—paragraphs that set out the process of resumption and the manner in which compensation would be determined, and then in obscure legalese, an outline of what legal rights Minnie, as the owner, would have. The letter contained so much information to absorb that it took Deedee a good ten minutes to read, review and reread, all the while Minnie sat silently, rubbing her hands together. Merlin, who had followed Deedee into the parlour, rubbed himself against Minnie's ankles almost as if trying to provide some measure of comfort—but it didn't appear to be working.

Setting the letter down, Deedee spoke. 'I think the first thing we need to do is speak to a lawyer about what we can do to challenge this decision. I suppose you still use the local solicitor?' Seeing Minnie's nod, she continued, 'Well then, I'll ring him and see if I can send him a copy of this letter and make a time to go and see him.' With increasing anger in her voice, she continued, 'I also need to make another call. I'm pretty sure I know who is behind all of this. You stay here by the fire; I'll make those calls and come back with a pot of tea. You've had a shock—you need a hot drink and maybe something sweet to go with it. Don't move.'

Minnie's lack of objection to being ordered around, was a true measure of her distress. She just nodded and sat staring into the fire. Merlin jumped onto the newly vacated spot and settled beside his mistress.

Deedee's phone calls were brief and to the point. An appointment was made with the solicitor for the following morning, and she promised to email them a scanned copy of the correspondence straight away. Her call to Julian went straight to voice mail, so she was forced to leave a message—not a calm, measured message, but one full of concern.

'What's going on? I've just got home to find my great-aunt in tears as a result of a letter from the council. What have you done?'

There was nothing more she could do at this stage except calm her aunt and try to calm herself. She focussed on boiling the kettle and laying out the tray with her aunt's best cups and saucers, and a plate of dainty shortbread. A refrain rattled over and over in her head. *Surely this cannot be possible. No point expecting Minnie to do anything. It was up to her. She must stop it from happening. But how?*

Chapter Twenty-Three

Even though nothing had changed, the ritual of tea drinking somehow settled both women. The knowledge that they would be consulting their local solicitor the following morning eased Minnie's anxiety somewhat. Perhaps he could act as an intermediary in any contact with the council. She could pass over the burden and leave it to him to fight on her behalf. The thought of losing her home and all the memories associated with it, was far more painful to her than she had ever anticipated as she had always hoped to hand it over to her great-niece. Although she knew her time here was ending, Minnie had always drawn comfort from the thought that this, her home, would continue to protect and inspire others, her great-niece, and maybe one day more children could be raised in the security of these protective surroundings. Now, it looked like plans were underway to turn this refuge into an expanse of asphalt, with kerb and guttering. A necessary evil no doubt, but did it have to be here?

The fire crackled, the cat purred, and silence otherwise descended on the small room as both women were lost in their own thoughts. The rising wind outside heralded an approaching storm, but they ignored it, thoughtfully sipping tea and staring into the flickering flames.

A bang on the front door startled them.

'I'll get it,' said Deedee, jumping up from the lounge and heading out into the corridor towards the front door. Upon opening the door, she stepped back and abruptly announced, 'Oh, it's you. I suppose you need to come in. I think you owe us an explanation.'

It was Julian. He shook his umbrella, closed it, and left it by the front door before moving past Deedee and into the corridor.

'What awful weather. It came in from the south in a rush. Luckily, I had this brolly in the car. I came as soon as I got your message. I really don't know what you are on about by the way, but if I can help, of course I will.'

'I should hope so,' Deedee muttered darkly, ushering Julian into the parlour. Before she could introduce him, her aunt started upright in shock.

'Not you again. I suppose you and your family are behind this letter?' she said, scrabbling for the letter that had only recently been left on the coffee table. 'Where has it got to? It was here just a moment ago.' Minnie's hands shifted through the debris that all coffee tables attract—old magazines, correspondence and other reading materials.'

'Here it is Aunt,' said Deedee, holding the letter aloft and passing it over to Julian who gave it a cursory glance.

'Ummm,' he said.

'Is that all you can say?' demanded Deedee. 'Surely this is your doing or that of your family?'

'Well, not exactly. We did suggest in our subdivision application that access through this block would provide the safest means of access. You know—a wide, double lane, boulevard type entrance? That would enhance the nature of the development and promote ease of traffic flow,' he said, sounding like someone reading from a real estate brochure. 'Looks like they took our suggestion to heart,' he continued, once more glancing down and rereading the letter. He looked up and regarded the two glowering women. 'It makes sense, you know. And this house is falling down around your ears. If we left it a few more years, it would be rubble. Just now I nearly fell through a hole on the front verandah.'

'That's because we are rebuilding it and it is not yet finished. It is not falling down—well, not yet anyway,' Deedee conceded.

'If you had just listened to me earlier Mrs Green,' Julian said, his eyes looking beseechingly at Minnie, who gave no response. 'If you'd just listened to me and accepted my offer, we wouldn't be in this situation. You could have continued to live out your time here while we started on the subdivision. It's going to take years to do, and it will be quite a while till the final access is required.'

The subtext on this comment was not lost on any of them— that by the time the subdivision would be almost complete, Minnie would be long dead. Deedee bristled in indignation. How dare he! Before she could say anything, Minnie launched into a diatribe.

'It's not happening. Do you hear me? This is more than our home. This is local history. It is as much a historic monument to our early days as the town hall or the church up there on the hill. I will not allow it, do you hear? I have friends and they will support me.' Minnie drew herself up to her full height—not much in reality and probably not as intimidating as the sparks that flew from her furious eyes. Yet somehow the effect was strangely intimidating as she stood all a quiver, arm fully extended, pointing at Julian. The black cat stretched and stood up on the lounge, back arched and eyes glaring at Julian. Grouped together like that, Minnie and her companion made an imposing sight.

'Alright, I get it. You're not happy and you're going to fight this order. Fair enough. It's your right to object, but it won't get you anywhere. I did try to be reasonable, remember? And I offered you good money, but you wouldn't listen. So, this is the result. And chances are your compensation will be so much less than what I offered.' With a casual shrug, he made his lack of sympathy very clear.

'That's it!' Minnie's voice rose to a screech. 'Get out of here. You're nothing but trouble. I never want to see you again!'

The lights flickered, the fire flared and in the shadows the faces of two very irritable old ladies appeared out of the wallpaper. But only Deedee noticed their arrival. Minnie and Julian were focussed on each other—the tall, dark, and slightly ominous looking, yet damp, man stood over the frail woman, who was bristling with rage.

The message to Eloise and Cicely was clear. Their Minerva

needed help and with the ammunition available to them, they went into battle. The light overhead flared and dimmed, and the fire flared even higher. One after the other, the china ornaments on the mantlepiece above the fire flew off in the direction of Julian. The first one was a direct hit, bouncing off his cheek. The second landed directly on his forehead.

'Ouch! Who did that? That's not funny, you know. Stop it. Do you hear?' he said, looking around for the culprit as yet another ornament flew through the air and hit him on the chest.

Minnie's fury dissipated. She was not alone. She had support. Even though she was not attached to the ornaments that now lay shattered on the rug, the thought of having to clean it up made her decide to call a halt to the proceedings. After all, the situation was now becoming rather farcical—this tall and wild-looking, demonic being brought undone by two grumpy spirits.

'You need to get out of here—now!' Minnie ordered. 'I think this house and its otherworld inhabitants have made it clear that you are not welcome. You need to go before they start casting fireballs at you.'

A rusty cackle could be heard, like something drifting in from far away.

'Don't give them ideas Aunt,' pleaded Deedee. It was definitely possible that those horrible old ladies would do something like that. Given their skill with hurling china, who knew what else they would throw?

Julian backed away, eyes wide with terror.

'I'm out of here. I don't do ghosts. Now I am even more convinced this house must go. And there's nothing that will stop me.'

He headed out into the corridor, made his way to the front door, and wrenched it open. For a moment he stared out into the pelting rain and hesitated. Then, with a glance back to the parlour and the flaring light within, he turned and moved out through the door.

Deedee grabbed the umbrella and went after him.

'Don't forget this. It won't be much help in all that, but I don't want anything of yours left here. Go and never, ever talk to me again. I can't believe you have been so conniving.'

Julian turned around once more and with an almost pleading look, he said, 'I'm sorry, but you just don't understand.'

That did it. She didn't understand. Surely he had that the wrong way around. *He* didn't understand what this home meant to all of them—living *and* dead!

Through gritted teeth, Deedee spoke. 'Just go and I hope I never see you again!'

Julian turned and left as the door slammed shut. Whether it was the wind that drove it shut or her angry shove, she neither knew nor cared. The hurt and rage insider her coalesced and for a moment she contemplated running after Julian and screaming her anger at him—or worse. Her aunt's call brought her to her senses—just— but she was a quivering mess when she returned to the parlour. Minnie, taking one look at her distraught great-niece, spoke.

'Wine. Now! Or something stronger if you think it best. For medicinal purposes only, you understand? And by the look of you, you might need the entire bottle.'

Deedee barely heard Minnie. Her mind was still racing, contemplating what had just occurred. Then, looking around, she considered the mess that lay scattered around them.

'But what about this mess? Shouldn't we tidy it up?'

'Well, I never liked those ornaments much anyway,' said Minnie. 'And I guess Eloise and Cicely didn't either. Maybe cleaning up the mess can keep till the morning. Who knows, maybe the old dears will tidy up after themselves.'

Was that a distant snort that Deedee could hear?

'Priorities, Deedee dear. The wine. I think we've earned it and maybe we need to settle our nerves as we could be in for a wild night. They both tilted their heads to one side as they listened to the rain still pelting on the tin roof. The noise was so loud that it was hard to hear anything else. A crack of thunder and simultaneous flash of lightning overrode the sound of the rain—a sign the storm must have been overhead. Merlin screeched and flew out of the room, but with the sound of another even louder *crash* and *thud*, he returned as if he had been chased back towards them.

The noise made the remaining ornaments on the mantlepiece rattle and the house jolt.

'My goodness. That was something being hit by lightning. A tree maybe? And by the sounds of it, somewhere nearby. Only something close could have made such an impact. Maybe the elm?' Minnie said, clutching at her throat. 'I'm not going out there to see if it was that tree. At least it missed the house. Now where's that wine?'

They sat and drank in silence, each lost in their own thoughts. Finally, Minnie summed up her feelings by saying, 'Dearest great-niece, what will be, will be. So many lives lived in this house. We owe it to them to go down fighting. I don't like our chances, but I sure as hell won't give up. Let me propose a toast. Here's to another David and Goliath battle!'

They clinked glass and exchanged smiles. Round one had been a disaster, but the enemy had been driven away—even if only temporarily. But maybe, somehow it would be possible to do so forever.

Chapter Twenty-Four

The storm continued in sound and fury all night. From time to time, Deedee would stir awake, register the ongoing clatter of water raining on the roof, the creak and rattle of roofing iron and timbers as the house resisted the assault by the wind, then she would roll over and slip back into sleep—deep and dreamless. Drained by the trauma of the day, all her body needed was rest and repair. She only fainted registered Merlin jumping onto her bed in the wee small hours and snuggling into the crook of her knees. Other than adjusting her position to accommodate his bulk, his arrival did little to disturb her slumber.

The storm had blown itself out by morning and Deedee awoke to a world washed clean. The patch of sky visible from her bedroom window was a clear duck egg blue. There was not a cloud to be seen. She was awoken early by Merlin pawing at her face with a gentle, but insistent, movement.

'Okay. Okay. I get it. You need to go outside. Let me get dressed and we will both go and inspect the damage.'

Both cat and human left the house through the side door and contemplated an almost unrecognisable garden. Where once the garden had been awash with blossom and blooms, there was now a carpet of finely shredded leaves and flowers. Shrubs, torn apart as if by a whirlwind, hung in abject surrender. Deedee carefully walked along the garden path, taking care not to slip on the leaves strewn along the way. She headed towards the heart of the garden—Bertie's territory—where a sheltering elm once stood sending its branches out like so many protective arms. But it was no longer. In complete shock, Deedee contemplated the stark remains of the once majestic tree. Her aunt was correct. It was a lightning strike, and a massive one at that, to have damaged the tree so badly. The thud they heard must have been the sound of the bulk of the trunk hitting the ground once it was sheared by a direct hit from the lightning. A good two thirds of the tree lay splintered and scattered across the garden, other smaller trees also having been crushed as it fell. Broken branches and shucked leaves were strewn in a random mess. The trunk had fallen heavily along the path and lay in one solid piece. With all the mess of destroyed vegetation, it wasn't possible for Deedee to get any closer to the destroyed tree and, in the face of such destruction, she found herself not even wanting to. Was this a portend of the future for her home? When bulldozers eventually appeared and flattened everything, the land would look something like this small patch of garden—flattened and bearing no resemblance to its former appearance. If that was what the future held, she wanted to be far away so that the image of such destruction would not linger in her catalogue of memories.

It was time to wake her aunt and inform her of the damage. It was sad news that she didn't want to convey, but she needed to. As she turned, a glint of something reflecting the sunlight caught her eye—a glint along the path hidden by tangled branches, next to the broken tree trunk. Moving carefully, she stepped around twigs, branches and debris until she got as close as possible. It was still more than a metre away. She could see that what had attracted her attention was something metal—like a fan of metal chopsticks with some shredded remnants of a waterproof nylon fabric attached to them. Her stunned brain took a moment to process the item, but she soon realised she had seen it as recently as the night before when she had shoved it at the departing Julian. It was an umbrella, or rather the remains of what was once an umbrella.

As the significance of the presence of this umbrella in among the debris dawned on her, her angry parting words to Julian echoed in her mind '*I hope I never see you again,*' she had yelled at his departing back. Could it be that she had sealed his fate with those words?

She looked closer and there, near the debris, but closer to the tree trunk, was something else—something leather and black. Squinting, she tried hard to focus on the image. It took a while as the area was a mix of sunlight and shadow, making identification a bit more of a challenge. Then, with dawning horror, she realised that what she was staring at was a foot—shod in a stylish black riding boot. It was a boot she recognised, having seen it only the day before. Deedee backed away, eyes wide with horror. The foot hadn't moved, and it was beyond any imagining that a person would survive after being struck by such a massive tree. She needed to get help and wake her aunt. As she walked carefully back to the house, she could not help but give a small smile, despite her feelings of shock. She had been worrying about telling Minnie about the destruction of her garden, but now she had to inform her about the destruction of their enemy. Somehow though, she thought that may not be altogether unwelcome news.

The emergency services were quick in arriving. The news that there might have been a fatality seemed to give their job priority over the many other calls they had no doubt received. A group of men and women in orange overalls emblazoned with 'SES' on the back appeared with chainsaws in hand. Deedee led them to the damage and pointed out the shredded umbrella and well shod boot that was poking out of the tangled mess. The head person, a man she vaguely recognised, spoke to her.

'We can't do anything here until the police arrive. This is going to take a while. I'll send the rest of my gang onto the next job, but I'd better wait until the cops get here. Not sure how they are going to want to take things. Whether they'll let us get on with cutting up the mess to access whoever it is, or they may need to process things.'

The police arrived soon after and procedures were set in train. Deedee and her aunt were escorted into the house and asked to give statements. In the meantime, photos were taken of the site and steps taken to retrieve the body. To the background whine of a chorus of chainsaws, Deedee and her aunt gave their statements to two different police officers in separate rooms. Their stories were consistent as they outlined exactly what had happened. How Julian had come over in response to Deedee's call, how they had disagreed with him over his family's plan to develop the adjoining land and encourage the council to resume their home, and finally how they had sent him away.

'Into the storm?'

'Well, it was only raining at that stage and he had an umbrella,' Deedee explained. 'Anyway, he wanted to leave. There was nothing more to be said. It was only after he had left—a few minutes after actually—that we heard the thunder and saw the lightning. It didn't cross my mind that he would still be in the garden. Surely with that rain he would have run back to his car?'

*

A call from outside distracted them both. With a quick, 'excuse me', the officer left the room and headed back into the garden. A body, now under a sheet and on a stretcher, was being carried out of the yard to the side gate, where a waiting ambulance was parked. Most of the tree trunk had now been chopped into rounds and rolled onto the adjoining garden beds. Deedee, following the police officer out of the room, joined her aunt who was standing in the doorway, her distress obvious by the way she tightly clutched herself. Was she distressed about Julian or about the garden—or both?

'I never thought I would see such tragedy in this garden. I always thought of it as a place of refuge, not a place of death. Not that I liked the man, he was a bit creepy. That time he snuck up on me in the garden—well, it gave me a massive fright I tell you! Still, I wouldn't have wished this upon him.'

They were distracted by a call from the workers still cutting up remnant branches from the elm tree, and they moved as close as they could until their progress was halted, having been impeded by the chequered police tape.

'Here, over here by the tree roots. There's something else—bones, I think. The tree roots have kinda wrapped around them, so they are partly hidden. Where are the cops? We need them again.'

Deedee and her aunt stared at each other. Bones? Under the tree? They could only belong to one person. The person that lingered in that part of the garden and had been Deedee's childhood friend.

'Bertie?' Deedee whispered to her aunt.

Minnie nodded.

'Now we know why he chose that part of the garden as his own. It did belong to him after all. We may never know, but maybe he had some hand in what happened to Julian last night. After seeing how those old ladies behaved in the parlour, nothing would surprise me!'

*

The chaos of police and chainsaws lingered for days. It was only after they left that the two ladies realised their lives had changed forever. The landscape of the garden was denuded of greenery and the massive sheltering tree. It was not only bare and bleak, but also strangely silent. The bird life had moved to other more hospitable gardens and a certain boy child ghost was now absent. His bones had been removed and his spirit no longer lingered.

Deedee consoled her great-aunt. It was clear she had taken the recent events to heart and was struggling.

'Minnie, it will all come back. We'll get Harry to help with replanting and before you know it you will have your oasis again. And as for Bertie, in some ways it will be a relief not to have him and his mischievous ways. At least you will now be able to keep track of your gardening tools. Maybe once he is buried with his family, he too can find peace. Mind you, I think I will miss him.'

The two women, separated in age by many years but linked by

genetics and mutual regard, smiled lovingly at each other. Linking arms, they headed back to their sheltering home, followed by a black feline who, pausing for an instant, looked back to where the elm had once grown. He had what could almost be considered a look of triumph in his glowing eyes.

*

Chapter Twenty-Five
Twelve Months Later

It was a typical day in late spring, the weather flicking between sunny, cloudy, showery, and blustery—over and over. It had been a day Deedee had been dreading for some time as her aunt slowly faded away. Yet now that it was here and the funeral service was over, she felt much better—almost at peace. The small, red brick church was filled to capacity as the local residents gathered to honour Minnie's life and acknowledge her contribution to the close-knit community.

Deedee welcomed the support Harry and his family had provided. Seated on either side of her, they filled the entire pew. Harry sat to her right holding her hand gently, and every now and then he would check to see if she was coping. His parents and siblings were on her other side, their comforting solidity providing reassurance. This was her only family now. A family that had become hers as she settled into a life with Harry. It was an added and unexpected benefit because she now had no blood relatives left in the world—or at least none that she knew of.

Minnie had been adamant that she would be cremated, telling anyone that cared to listen that she found the thought of being buried under cold, damp earth horrifying. 'What if I'm still alive?' she would say. 'That would be beyond my worst nightmare. Make sure I'm cremated, and you can scatter me on my garden where I belong—with living things—not in a cemetery with dead bones.'

So that is exactly what Deedee had arranged. Once the service was over and the coffin was left standing before the altar—virtually invisible under its mantle of spring blossoms—Deedee and the congregation left the church. There was no need for her to accompany the coffin to the crematorium and indeed Deedee didn't feel like she could. Whatever was left of Minnie was not lingering in that wooden box. Now that her living and breathing aunt was long gone, Deedee found she could let go of the physical body that Minnie had once occupied. For what actually mattered—the love and joy in life that Minnie had in abundance—was still with her, held closely inside Deedee, in her memories and in the values that her great-aunt had so diligently instilled in her.

Standing outside the church, and still flanked by Harry and his parents, Deedee tried to respond appropriately to the kind words of condolence she received. In recent months, she had seen how much Minnie meant to the people of the small town just by their regular visits to bring food, flowers or simply to provide comfort with their physical presence. She thought that it should ease her pain to know that her sense of loss was shared by so many others—but somehow it didn't.

A wake of sorts was to be held at a local café—tea, scones and sandwiches. Deedee explained to those who spoke to her that she would catch up with them there, and soon—too soon—she saw them drift away, lured by the promise of food and the chance for a good gossip.

Clutching a few mismatched blooms she had taken from the church nave, Deedee turned away.

'Come on Harry. There's one thing to do before we go and join the others at the wake—something we should both do today.'

Taking Harry by the arm, she led him away—past the church and out behind where the cemetery stood in wonky disarray. So many of the headstones were unidentifiable, their details worn away by time and the weathering of countless storms. Today though, that was not an issue as Deedee knew exactly where she was headed. Towards the back of the cemetery, near a sheltering windbreak of aged pines whose branches, weighed down with age and possible weakness, leaned down to almost touch the tallest of the stone memorials. There, in what was obviously a family plot, was a starkly new headstone, white and shiny in contrast to its neighbours. Bending down, Deedee carefully lay the flowers across the mound of dirt and stood back considering the grave. Harry drew Deedee towards him as they stood in silent contemplation. Moments passed. Shoulder to shoulder, the two people stood gazing down at the small grave.

'I like to think he is at peace now, next to his mother and his sisters. Do you think he really is?'

'Well, he's left the garden now and I suppose that means something. For some reason he wasn't settled back in the garden and I sometimes wonder if he had a role in revealing his bones to us—so we could bring them back to his family. Yes, I really do think young Bertie might finally be at peace. You know, I never thought I'd miss him moving my gardening tools, but to my surprise I do.'

Deedee reached into her pocket and withdrew a small figure—a carved wooden bird. Tracing her fingers along the outline of the head, beak and wings, she spoke.

'The gift of this little bird saved me when I was so lost and alone all those years ago, and for so long I have kept it as a sort of talisman—a good luck charm. But maybe I've grown out of that need. I think my good luck is what I make it, and maybe it's time to return this bird to Bertie.'

Bending down she carefully nestled the small carved creature into the loose dirt at the base of Bertie's headstone, then gently patted the soil around it so it would rest securely.

'There, that's done. Another ending.' She stood and faced Harry, staring intently into those deep green eyes.

'All those years ago, it was you and Bertie who were the saving of that little lost soul that was me. I don't think I ever thanked you at the time, but I certainly was grateful. I don't know what would have happened to the child that I was if it hadn't been for you and Bertie.'

'And Minnie and Alice—don't forget them. We were *all* there when you needed us. And I still am if you ever need me, but somehow, I suspect that won't be necessary. You've seen the demons off, saved your cottage—with the assistance of community outrage of course—and you are now transforming and heading into an amazing future as a landscape artist. That last bit, however, is due to my input, I should say in all modesty.' Harry's eyes twinkled. Pulling her close, he kissed Deedee gently on the forehead, and continued: 'Dearest Deedee. Well done. I'm sure Minnie and Alice, wherever they are, will be cheering you on to your next adventure. Mind you, if they don't start, I will soon be nagging you to finish that book. What was it called again? *Minerva and her Magic Garden?*'

About the Author

Once a lawyer Dorothy now writes full time. She likes to write about the things that interest her – old houses, gardens, animals and occasionally about ghosts.

Dorothy lives in Tasmania in a romantic stone Georgian house with a long-suffering husband and a menagerie of animals.

Other stories by Dorothy may be found on Amazon Kindle.